I DO NOT BELONG

RICK WOOD

ABOUT THE AUTHOR

Rick Wood is a British writer born in Cheltenham.

His love for writing came at an early age, as did his battle with mental health. After defeating his demons, he grew up and became a stand-up comedian, then a drama and English teacher.

He now lives in Loughborough with his fiancée, where he divides his time between watching horror, reading horror, and writing horror.

ALSO BY RICK WOOD

The Edward King Series:

Book One – I Have the Sight
Book Two – Descendant of Hell
Book Three – An Exorcist Possessed
Book Four – Blood of Hope
Book Five – The World Ends Tonight

The Sensitives:

Book One – The Sensitives
Book Two – My Exorcism Killed Me
Book Three – Close to Death
Book Four – Demon's Daughter

Standalones:

When Liberty Dies

Sean Mallon:

Book One – The Art of Murder

Cover design by rickwoodswritersroom.com

Copy-edited by LeeAnn @ FirstEditing.com

With thanks to my Street Team

This book is dedicated to those of you who do not belong.

You know who you are.

"While I thought I have been learning how to live, I have been learning how to die."

Leonardo Da Vinci

"Why should I fear death? If I am, death is not. If death is, I am not. Why should I fear that which cannot exist when I do?"

Epicurus

"The boundaries which divide Life from Death are at best shadowy and vague. Who shall say where one ends, and the other begins?"

Edgar Allen Poe

THE ONE WHO DOESN'T BELONG

I was bored.

I guess you could say that's why I did it.

Or, that I'm fascinated. Completely overcome by a desire to know more, to know what it's like, how it feels – to truly experience it myself.

You see it every day in the news, don't you?

Predators picking off easily coerced children, tempting them with a frivolous treat, prying them away from easily distracted mothers who wouldn't watch their kids with their full attention but would cry on the television appeal.

Oh, the irony. Honestly, they deserve the scare, just to teach them to watch the child that they apparently want back so sodding much.

Wah wah wah, cry cry cry, my child my child my child – shut up, you stupid cow, no one cares. Sure, everyone cares about your missing kid for this minute, but then they press the red button, turn off the news, and carry on with their equally repugnant lives. Flush the memory away after tutting for a fleeting second, like that picture of your kid you printed on your t-shirt actually makes a single bit of difference to them. Your child is the discarded milk carton from the previous day's cereal – not that that's actually a thing anymore, missing kids on milk cartons. It's more 'missing kids on Facebook' now. Normally as their mother's profile picture. Like that does anything. Put them wherever you want, you inept cow: you weren't watching them, so someone took them, you're a shit mum.

And that's the thing – that very thing that enthrals me. The reason behind it.

Why?

Why would you do that? Why portray yourself as the doting parent and let your kid go astray with some fucking weirdo?

But, in all honesty, it's not the mothers that fascinate me. They are fascinating, yes, but it's not them. It is the artists behind it that make me want to know more.

And, honestly, that's why you watch the news. Isn't it? Not because you care. Because you are fascinated, just like me. Intrigued by what the artist has done, and who the artist may be, and whether or not the artist is too elusive to be caught.

And I am a fucking weirdo, let's not pretend I'm not. You may not realise it fully yet, but that's only because you are yet to witness what I've done. Once you've read the book, you will think – no, you will know – I am a *fucking weirdo*.

And you are a *fucking weirdo*.

And you don't even realise it.

And you don't know why.

And that brings me back to the *why* you so ardently demand:

Human behaviour captivates me.

It seems, no matter the situation, no matter the stakes, the cost, the person – put someone in a position where they are against another with their life at stake, and they will be a bastard.

All people are bastards.

Even you.

Let's be honest; who are you in it all for?

Your spouse? Your kids? You parents? Siblings? Friends?

No.

You are in it for you.

Come on, admit it.

It's just between us. No one will know.

You don't even need to say it aloud. Your partner asleep in the bed next to you, or your sibling across the room, your friends on Facebook, your parents shoved away in an old people's home to rot – they won't hear your thoughts. So you can be honest. Finally, you can be absolutely, crucially, unequivocally, diabolically honest.

You're a bastard, too. Aren't you?

I want you to answer that question. Now.

Aren't you?

Answer it. AREN'T YOU?

...

Thank you. Whether consciously intentional, or subconsciously unaware, you will have given me a yes or no.

And one of two things will have happened in your response.

Either you will have responded with, "Yeah, I guess I am," completely agreed and concurred that you are, too, in fact, undeniably, a bastard.

Or you have just lied to yourself.

Easy to do, I guess. But hey, that's your prerogative. It's up to you what truth you wish to perceive.

For me, I chose four people – four supposedly undefeatable, shiny beams of light – and I let them tear each other apart. Destroy each other. I thought, putting myself amongst them, I'd have to do more talking, coercing, manipulating, pushing. As it was, I got away with saying and doing very little to move the situation along.

Being the bastards they are, whether underneath or on the surface – they did exactly as I expected.

And boy, are they bastards.

Like you.

Just wait. You'll see.

You may, on occasion through their story, question whether you would do the same. Whether the actions they take would be the same as yours within the scenario put forward to you in this story. Maybe there's one character you identify with more, or one you hate, or one you take a particular liking to as a relationship grows. Maybe someone's backstory convinces you of that character's noble intentions, or complete and utter ruthlessness. Maybe you even choose to root for one to be the killer. Maybe you even guess who I am. Maybe you get it right, maybe you don't. Maybe you're certain, or maybe you just sit back, shut the hell up, and read the sodding book.

Remember, whatever your thoughts – you would act no differently.

And hey, I'll be straight with you.

I'm a regular bastard too – except more so.

Because I've embraced it.

And to consider yourself above any of the beautifully terrible people would be delusional. It would be void of reality. Void of truth, and void of logic.

And, what's more, to convince yourself you're above me and my actions would be preposterous.

I'm not a psychopath. I don't have a personality disorder. Nor did I have a terrible childhood that scarred me for life and produced the monster you may accuse me of being. To relinquish the role of my character to any of these traits would be to demean my genius and what I seek to accomplish.

It would also demean my likeness to the average person.

Your average Joe.

Your regular nobody.
You.
I am you, except more so.
Remember that.

♌ 2 ♐

o HOURS, o MINUTES

A small shaft of light graces the room with its presence, fluttering through an irrelevant crack with such vague illumination that it does nothing to endow the scene with clarity. Despite being the only natural light to creep into the room, it is so insignificant and so miniscule that none of the characters you are about to meet discover it. There is a fake light flickering overhead, like you would stereotypically expect in a neglected corridor, or an abandoned warehouse, or a piss-stinking bathroom at a run-down garage in the middle of nowhere.

That flickering light in itself is so artificial it would make your mind burst against your skull. It has a strong orange tint, like someone had peeled a satsuma, turned it into a transparent material able to filter light, and fixed it against the bulb.

Five figures lay dormant upon the faded tiles. A chain around each right ankle secures their positions with an inescapable security. There are a few metres of give on their chain, but ultimately, they are confined to the small radius that the chain allows them. They will be able to move, yes – but none of them will be able to leave; not only are they confined by their restraints, but there is no visible door that makes a route out obvious. It is a room with no windows, no apparent exit, no visible means of escape.

The interior of the room is a cross between a filthy kitchen and an unconventional basement that one never enters. In truth, it is a bomb shelter, built out of paranoia, but one so neglected that you would not recognise it for such a use any more than you would recognise shredded felt as the teddy bear such material originally created. The crackling walls display feverous mould, over a floor that's once startling decoration is now reduced to mossy imprints, covered by dirt engraved for such a long time it has become as much a part of the surface as the floor's immovable cracks. An unidentifiable drip creates an irritating ambience – an irritating ambience which grows even more irritating when entwined with the hollow reverberation that mimics any of the room's ill-fated guests, transforming all small sounds to a suffocation of the ears. As our protagonists begin to stir, their shuffles repeat back in a vast echo caused by the walls, floor, and ceiling of the metallic box.

One by one they wake. One by one they panic. One by one they look at each other, terrified of what is going on.

It would be boring to describe to you the sheer mortification of each waking character individually, and for you to have to experience it five times, so I will spare you the unneeded details. After all, you are not stupid – you can make the assumption that if you were to wake up in a random room that felt like a knapsack, with four strangers, with your ankle fixed to the floor, you would be equally horrified; so to describe each character's independent adjustment to the awful situation they find themselves in would be to patronise you and waste your time. It would be obviously safe to presume that each of these people woke with a start, a scream, and eyes wide with terror. That their bodies trembled like a ship caught in a storm, and their tears were just as wet as said ship's deck, and their stomachs just as sickly as any passenger on said rocky ship. That their thoughts ran through a hundred vile possibilities of why they may be there: sexual slavery, torture, perversion, monotonous curiosity, sadistic thrills, or to simply give their captor a raging erection. And, in all honestly, I couldn't say that any of those possibilities would be right or wrong.

But let's not waste your time with all that needless description of how their hearts are racing, how their blood is pumping, how they think of those they love, yada yada yada, blah blah blah.

Let's just see how the scumbags get on, all right?

"What's going on?" barks the Liverpudlian accent of a black man in his early twenties as he pulls on the chains that clamp around his ankle. His name is Ashley, and he does everything he can to push his bondage off, but unfortunately it does not move. "Where am I?"

The young girl next to him, merely sixteen years old, a college student already facing withdrawal symptoms from her anxiety medication, backs away from him like an animal scared of an intruder. Her arms shake so furiously you could be mistaken for believing a tornado is surging through her bones. Her face is so full of perspiration she has to keep blinking beads of sweat out of her eyes, and her head won't stop twitching.

"Hey," Ashley says, offering a hand toward her. "Cool down."

She doesn't cool down. She stares at his hand like he's offering her shit on fire, and backs up against the wall.

His head pounds with the throbbing of a monstrous hangover – the kind of hangover that would reduce God himself to a quivering wreck, laid out on the sofa with a flannel on his face, demanding to be left alone.

"Hey," Ashley continues, holding one hand out to the girl, the other on his head that feels like something is drilling into his skull. "It's cool. I don't know what I'm doing here either."

Her bottom lip trembles with the ferocity of a washing

machine on full spin. She is unknowingly drooling, a large gunk of saliva hanging from her mouth, but she is slowly discovering that Ashley is not the enemy.

"My name's Ashley. What's yours?"

"M – M – Maya," she replies.

"Maya, that's a nice name. Do you know who put you here, Maya?"

She stares at him, considering his question, then shakes her head with a rabid fever, which then prompts tears to glisten in her eyes then shoot down her cheeks.

Ashley turns and looks at the others. All of them cautiously move their eye contact from one another, never meeting each other's gaze. Extreme trepidation takes hold of their composure. All of them cautious, wary of the others.

That is, all except one.

A man sat in the corner glares at Ashley. He is in his late sixties, and there are things about Ashley this man does not like.

"What's your name?" Ashley asks.

"Fuck off," the man replies. His name, however, is not fuck off – it is Milo Clunk.

Ashley turns his attention to the other two. One a woman, the other a man.

"Do any of you know how you got here?" Ashley asks.

They shake their heads, eyes wide, blubbering messes.

Ashley looks at their ankles. Everyone is restrained with the same immovable force he is.

The girl next to him is still blubbering. Ashley tunes it out.

"Right, let's be cool, let's figure out why we're here. What are your names?"

"Tariq," replies the man. Late forties, a Muslim immigrant, proud owner of a pharmacy. His voice is kind, his accent a cross between his Bangladeshi heritage and his many years living in the United Kingdom.

"Everly," replies the woman. In her early thirties, attractive enough that she would turn heads as she walked down the street. Except now she is less so – sweaty, with hair greased back, and some kind of contraption around her neck.

"What is that?" Ashley asks, pointing at said contraption.

Everly looks down and sees the device. She panics. Starts screaming. Starts shaking. Dancing around on the spot, like constant shifting will do anything to remove it. It won't – it's a large metallic necklace, fixed to her body via her collar bone, with a small gun set in place so that it is in front of her throat, pointed straight up at her chin. She grabs hold of the gun and tries to shift it, tries to point it somewhere else, to move it, but it's no good – it's welded in place. What's more, it's making a ticking noise, as if it is on a timer.

"What the fuck is happening?" she cries.

"I don't know," Ashley answers, staring at her unwanted necklace. Fresh paranoia makes him look down to see if he has one too, but he does not.

Tariq goes to have a look at it, and Ashley becomes suddenly startled by his back.

"Tariq!" Ashley says, pointing – then instantly regrets it, deciding it would have been a better idea not to have drawn attention to it.

Tariq fiddles with his back, and that's when he feels it. Something fixed to his spine.

Ashley immediately feels himself for a device on his body, running his hands over his neck, his back, his legs, his face. Nothing.

Maya has started doing the same, although with a lot more panic and a lot more tears. Ashley can see she's young, but wishes she would calm down. Her panic only escalates further, however, when she finds something over her heart. She lifts her raggedy vest to reveal a small metallic circle with a flashing red light stuck just above the left side of her bra, which is purple with large yellow dots on, and slightly too big for her flat chest.

Then Everly's eyes fix on Maya, and hold there, and she gasps.

"Oh my God, Maya!" she weeps.

"Auntie Everly?" the girl replies. "Auntie Everly, what's going on?"

Ashley turns to Milo.

"You got anything?" he asks.

Milo doesn't move from his slump against the wall, except to raise his middle finger and direct it at Ashley.

"You know, that ain't helpful, man. We're all here together for a reason, we got to figure it out."

Milo's middle finger remains strong.

"Fine. Let's try and figure out why—"

Ashley sees it. In the middle of the room. An envelope. Why hadn't he noticed this before?

He rushes forward and picks it up.

"Anyone know what this is?" Ashley asks.

Vague, empty faces answer him.

"Open it," Tariq requests.

Ashley opens it and withdraws a small note written on A5 lined paper.

He reads the letter aloud:

Hello, my friends.

Four of you have been selected to take part in today's activity. Four of you will have been placed here by me, the fifth one.

I am one of you.

Your task is to figure out which one of you I am.

You must all be agreed in your decision.

For every hour that you do not come to a correct and unanimous decision, one of you will die.

But you won't know who until the hour is up.

Over to you – can you figure out which one of us is the one who DOES NOT BELONG?

Good luck.

Ashley looks up. Stares at each person in turn. As does Tariq. Everly. Maya. Even Milo raises his head for a moment.

So one of them put them there?

And they have to figure out who.

"How long do we have?" Everly asks.

Ashley looks down. He wears a watch. A childish plastic watch with a red strap and a buckle that digs into his wrist. He has never seen this watch before.

"This watch is on a timer," he says. "It's been thirty-eight minutes so far."

I Do Not Belong.

I Do Not Belong.

I Do Not Belong.

I Do Not.

I Do.

I.

❧ 3 ❧

0 HOURS 40 MINUTES

Ashley is suspicious of everyone.

Milo, who sits without a care. Rests his back against the wall. He's too old to worry.

Maya, whose frantic commotion attracts their attention a little too much.

Tariq, who's eerily quiet.

Everly, who... Well, gives nothing away about herself. But that in itself makes him wonder.

He knows he needs to find a door. They must have gotten in there somehow, there is no way they just appeared, and if there is an entry, then surely, just surely, it should also be an exit.

Hoping not to attract the attention of the others, he looks around. Scans the walls. Scans the roof. Scans the floor.

It looks like a perfectly crafted metal box. The room becomes a suspect in itself – like the others, it gives nothing away. But he knows that the room must be hiding something.

Keeping his eyes on the others, he crouches, feels around the floor. His hands fall over the chain that trails from his ankle. Beneath that, metal. Nothing but rusty, prickly metal. He drags his hands over it, hoping to find something, some give-away, but all the floor produces is a long line of dust on his finger.

Then he looks behind himself.

There is a hole in the wall. Too small to attract attention. Too small for anyone else to notice. But he knows there wouldn't be a hole without a reason.

He peers at it. Doesn't get too close, doesn't want anyone else to know, but he sees it.

A small circle, not even big enough to fit a finger.

But it's a starting point.

He keeps his back to it. Watches everyone else.

Suspects everyone else.

They are all hiding something, and he knows it.

But then again, what is he hiding?

Because the one that put them there, the one in the room with them all, the one who does not belong – they know it.

They know what all of them are hiding.

And none of them are safe.

❧ 4 ❧

ASHLEY

I stare at the wall. A wall I should be proud of. A wall I want to tear down. Literally. I imagine my hands ripping into its plaster, punching through the outdated floral wallpaper like it was my meanest opposition, grabbing its guts and ripping it into strips barely recognisable from the sturdy horizontal display it once was.

It all means nothing. It's as permanent as wet paper. Easily ripped. Easily crumpled into a messy ball that misses the bin.

Ma was proud. She still is.

But then again, Ma doesn't know.

She doesn't know how I got these medals.

She erected the wall in dedication to me. She has a chair in front of it where she often sits, watching my trophies like you would a movie. Like they were an adequate replacement for me, idolising my memories as if they are more perfect than I am. As if those trophies were a far better thing to love than me, myself.

She thinks it's a compliment.

It ain't.

Silver medal. An Olympian. A champion boxer.

"Oh, Ashley," she says as she meanders toward me. "This wall makes me so proud."

She's a brilliant woman, my ma. She isn't getting any younger, but she still stands stronger than I do. She raised me all on her own, and I weren't no piece of cake to raise. I battled against her each and every day of my adolescence, went against every word she said, preferring to spend my time running around with mates who led me down a bad path, a path decorated with trees of crime and hate and anger; a path I would choose instead of the golden path she tried creating for me. Two of those lads I spent time with went to prison for gang crime, though I reckon they'd be out by now. Another's gone AWOL. And the other died of a knife attack almost three years ago. I miss them, but it weren't no life.

It was Ma who introduced me to my coach. I can't ever thank her enough for that. It showed me that amongst all the failed grades in class, the exclusions from school, the disappointed look from another teacher who saw me as nothing more than a letter on a piece of paper at the end of year 11 that either would or wouldn't stain their perfect record of exam results – that amongst all of this, there is something I am good at.

That's the great thing about boxing. When you've been fighting all your life and you finally get a chance to channel that fighting into something productive, you relish it – but there are rules. Any fighting on the street and you're out. Which meant having to say goodbye to a few good-for-nothings who did nothing for me.

Ma could have given me up. Lost it. The amount of times she was called into my school for another lecture on my behaviour and it did nothing but sadden her. The amount of silent drives home. The amount of nights I would watch her unnoticed from a crack in the door as she cried over another school report.

She could have given up on me so easily.

Said she couldn't handle it.

Send me to foster care.

Set me up for the early death I was battling toward.

But she didn't.

She stayed.

Kept me out of juvy.

Kept faith.

Still good old Ma.

"I wish you'd take it down," I tell her. "It's embarrassing."

"Embarrassing? Rubbish! I'm proud of what you've done. So should you be."

I ain't.

Because I didn't do any of it.

"Yeah," I sigh, drowning my head in my chest.

She wouldn't be so proud if she knew.

If she knew.

"Are you staying for tea?" she asks. I hear the optimism in her voice, the hope that I will stay. But I can't. I can't stay here with this... this wall of lies. I have to go.

"Nah, I got training," I tell her. It isn't strictly true, but I am going to head to the gym for a workout anyhow.

"Okay, dear, well, you take care."

She gives me a kiss and a hug and I tell her I love her and she tells me she loves me and it's all good. I could almost convince myself I'm worth her affections and her endless belief in me, her limitless convictions that I am the best thing to ever happen to her.

I could almost convince myself.

Almost.

I take to the streets and walk. Woolly hat on. Hood up. Don't know why. Just don't want to be seen.

People cross the road when they see me coming. A black

man with his hood up and his hands in his pockets. Obviously means I'm going to mug you. Idiots.

It's a full moon. Clouds creep across it like they are trying to conceal it from me. Like I ain't allowed its beauty. Like the moon only shines on people who deserve it.

They say the full moon brings out the crazies.

Well, tonight you'd be forgiven for thinking I am the crazy, such is the rabid look in my mortal eyes, my shaking as I feel withdrawal kicking in.

The gym is locked. Probably has been for hours. Doesn't matter, I know the code to the padlock on the backdoor. I go around and let myself in, turning the lights on in the changing room as I enter.

The main gym with the ring and the weights section is through the door. That's not where I go. I go to the toilets, shut the door to a cubicle and lock it.

Funny how, even when no one else is here, I still lock it. I still feel the need to be in secrecy. To hide this addiction from ghosts. From an absence of judging eyes that I still feel judging me nonetheless.

The needle meets my vein with the artistry of a seasoned painter. Far enough up my thigh that shorts will cover them. Funny, no one ever pays attention to a person's thigh, yet this is where people self-harm most. Where people have stretch marks, hidden wounds, war scars. Where I place the steroids in.

But isn't it always the hidden parts of us that are the most revealing, if also the most neglected?

I only just begin to press down on the needle when I hear a scuffle break out from across the changing room. I wrench the needle out with a sting and march through the changing room until I find him.

Before I even question how they got in, I feel a draught from the open door. Damn. I must not have locked it.

He rummages through the bins, a torn hat over a ripped

coat, rags hanging off bones, bags under eyes, and bloody veins across their pupils. They look at me like a rabid alley cat startled by a stranger.

"Oi!" I shout, making sure to be intimidating. "What the fuck you doin'?"

"Nothing," the person says defensively, glancing at the door, edging away from me. "I was just looking for stuff. Lookin'. Lookin' for..."

The man sees the needle still in my hand.

"Oh," the man says. His face moulds into an expression of recognition. "I know you."

The man looks from the needle to my face, to the needle, to my face; making the connections in his bedraggled mind.

"Oh. I see."

The disgusting hobo looks at what I'm doing, then looks at me like I'm the piece of shit.

I don't stop the man as he scuffles out, burying his head like he is ashamed to see what I'm doing, yet with a dishonourable triumph in his swagger. Like he is chuffed that he knows.

That he knows that I'm a fraud.

I look to the needle.

I hurl it across the room, but it doesn't smash. Doesn't break. Doesn't do anything but rebound off the wall and lay on the floor.

Something I'm glad of. Means I can still use it.

No. I don't want it.

God, how I don't want it.

It wasn't how I wanted to do this.

I wanted to conquer the world.

I wanted to–

I pick up the needle.

Who am I kidding?

I shut the back door and return to the bathroom cubicle.

5

o HOUR 58 MINUTES

Ashley's eyes fix on his plastic watch, watching each number change, the timer growing ever closer to the hour. He doesn't know what to expect. Why has he been given this watch? Is this a joke? Is someone actually going to die?

I mean, surely not.

They are all in an ominous, precarious position, yes – a terrifyingly twisted notion took over whoever came up with this concept, true – but surely, it's a prank? *Surely?*

I mean, these things only happen in horror movies.

Right?

"Two minutes," Ashley says, an apprehension in his voice that only begins to convey the nervousness fluttering around his stomach.

"You don't honestly think anything's actually going to happen, do you?" says Milo with a you're-so-pathetic-I-can't-believe-it voice.

Milo remains sat on the floor, slouched against the wall, contributing words that only serve to irk the others. His usefulness in helping them in the situation has so far been beyond nil.

If he'd have remained quiet that would have been unhelpful enough, but no; any time Ashley or Tariq has spoken he has started groaning, started muttering under his breath, the same bumbling noise. You couldn't deduce his words, but the hostility with which they have been grunted is undeniable. A handful of times he has shouted something that is just about audible, but nothing more useful than disparaging remarks instantly disregarded by the others; his three most pertinent contributions so far being, "Shut the fuck up I got a headache," "My arsecheek has gone so numb I'm starting to think the other one is eating it," and, "Are you all on acid you stupid patsies?"

He had been ignored so far, partly because no one understood what a patsy is – but with the time running out, they had no choice but to entertain the first relevant opinion he had volunteered.

"Seriously," he rambled on, "you lot are full of it."

"What you saying, you think it's all just a hoax?" Ashley asks.

"Don't know what it is, but it ain't got me worried," Milo says. "Only thing getting me going is being sat in here with you, porch monkey."

"What did you just call me?"

"Guys!" shouts Tariq, drawing Ashley and Milo's attention from what was the start of an inevitably long and drawn-out argument to direct their attention to Maya, who has suddenly started beeping.

Everly reaches her side and throws her arms around her young niece as quickly as she can. Maya's panicking has been so consistent for the last hour that, in all honesty, it had become white noise. But even though her desperate cries were nothing new, the cause made them all stiffen. Everly placed her arms around Maya, surprised there were any tears left in Maya's eyes to cry. But her cheeks, growing wrinkly from the damp, are adorned with even more streams of tears, travelling like a lake in a storm. Her whole body is convulsing in terror – not shaking or quivering, but vibrating with large thrusts, such is the fear taking control of her young body.

"It's okay, sweetie," Everly tells her, feeling sorry for the young girl. Who would do something so heartless to someone so young? "It's okay."

Maya rips her top open without a care for who sees what's underneath. The red light above her bra and over her heart now rhythmically flashes, accompanied by a ticking sound counting each second.

Everly places her hand over the flashing light, tries to rip it off, but only finds that the light is too deeply embedded; not just fixed into Maya's skin, but further into her rib cage. Everly begins to fear the metal necklace fixed to her neck, wondering if that will start ticking down next.

But no, she reassures herself, the letter is quite clear. One person would die every hour until they unanimously decided which one of them was causing this.

"What time we got?" Everly directs at Ashley.

Ashley looks at his watch. His eyes grow wide.

"Twenty-three seconds til the hour."

Maya screams a high-pitched piercing scream that resonates through their eardrums. She throws herself to the floor, wriggling like a seizing serpent, grabbing onto the light, peeling at it, yanking at it, doing everything she can but nothing at all.

Everly backs away.

This thing may have a blast radius, and she doesn't want to be caught in it.

It's not coming off. Everly can't argue with that – it is not coming off. There's nothing she can do. So she backs away. Takes care of herself. Let the teenager die.

It's not Everly's turn to die yet.

She knows it's her niece.

She knows she should do everything she can. That she should sacrifice her life if need be when it comes to protecting her family.

But she doesn't do any more than she has. She stays alive. Backs away as far as the chain around her ankle allows her.

You may interpret this act as callous or harsh, but that would only be if you aren't honest enough to realise that you'd doing nothing different. You, too, would let the child die her inevitable death to save you from your own, and you know it. After all, she may be your sister's child, but you don't owe her anything – and your sister will never know.

"Fifteen seconds."

Maya rolls around on the floor as if she's on fire, but accomplishes nothing. Her frantic state pushes her into a faint wooze, and she falls still, losing her conscious state in the final moments of her life.

"Whoever is doing this" – Everly shouts, looking to the others – "stop it!"

"Ten seconds."

"It's one of you, and you're going to kill her! Make it stop! Please, make it stop!"

"Five seconds."

"It could be you," Milo points out.

"Three."

"And it could be you!"

"Two."

Ashley stops counting down.

Everly meets his eyes. Worried, extreme concern peeling their eyelids wide open like invisible fishhooks had fallen from the roof and peeled them up.

The ticking stops.

The light ceases its flashing.

Maya's torso lifts into the air, a hand clutching her chest. She enters a seizure. Then she stops breathing.

"Does anybody know CPR?" Ashley asks.

Tariq looks around.

"I guess I know a little," he says.

"Are you a doctor?"

"No, a pharmacist."

"'Course you fuckin' are," Milo says with a shake of his head.

"What?" Ashley retaliates.

"All you fuckin' immigrants do is become doctors or pharmacists. An English fucker could have had that job."

"Shut up!" Everly shouts. "You are not helping!"

Tariq positions himself over the girl.

Her eyes are closed. Her body limp. Her face empty of expression.

Tariq does everything he can.

He places the heel of his right hand over the breastbone at the centre of Maya's chest. He places his other hand on top of his first hand and interlocks his fingers. He positions his shoulders over his hands.

He whispers a prayer.

Milo sneers at the sound.

Ashley keeps looking at his watch, following the time going by.

Tariq pounds on the girl's heart. Using his whole body weight to push down, again and again, then again and again, and again some more.

He takes a big breath, pinches her nose, covers her mouth with his, and breathes out.

He repeats this.

And he repeats his pounding on her heart.

And he repeats breathing into her mouth.

Mouth to mouth, pounding on her heart, clearing the airway, everything he can is not enough.

Eventually Tariq feels her pulse for the last time, and finds that it is still not there. He has no idea how much time has passed, but he knows he's been going at it for long enough. In an ideal situation, an ambulance would arrive and take over; there would be reason to keep going, keep trying, some salvation at the end of it. But there is nothing. Nothing but more empty attempts with empty results.

Ashley looks at his watch. Their time is going quickly.

Tariq stands.

"She's dead," he says.

Tariq, Ashley, and Everly bow their heads.

"Now there's four of us left," Ashley says, looking at his watch once more. "And we have just under forty minutes to figure out which one of us is doing this before someone else dies."

They all turn to Milo.

"And I'm starting to think I have an idea who it could be," says Ashley.

❧ 6 ❧

MAYA

I fucking *hate* my parents.

I hate them and I want to die.

Urgh!

So every other sixteen-year-old in the country is allowed to go out with their friends, but apparently not me. Want to know why? Because they are a bunch of DICKS. With a capital D, as well as a capital I, C, K, and S.

DICKS.

So I got off the phone to Jacey, and she said that her and the boys were going down the park – and she looks totally old so she can always get served which meant that there would be a couple of WKDs which is good as there's no way I'm going to get up and flirt with Steve and Andy without a bit of alcopop in me. I get ready, put on some makeup, some purple eyeshadow that's way more subtle than it sounds, and some lipstick of this shade that I saw in Boots when I was passing through to leave the Vic – I wouldn't normally shop in Boots, I'm not a povvo, nor am I a middle-class, middle-aged housewife.

Unlike my mum. The DICK.

Seriously, unless you are after Nurofen or something, go

somewhere else to buy your beauty products. The women in their beauty section look like frigging satsumas.

So as I was leaving the house, sneaking out the door and all that – not that I should have to, I'm sixteen, it's actually legal for me to fornicate, not that I planned to, I wasn't going to go and give it all straight away – maybe a cheeky blowy but nothing else – she came (my ugly, fat mum) and told me, "Dinner is ready!" (Not being funny, but I got too old to have dinner with my family when I was, like, twelve.)

I said I didn't want any and she said I was awfully dressed up and I said yeah, well, see you later. But then she stopped me and did the whole looking me up and down thing like she was judging me, like look at yourself bitch, you look like a repressed Victorian housewife dragged through a hedge backwards on fire. Her hair is greying and she pretends it isn't by getting highlights but it is greying and she won't admit it and it's just *so sad*.

"Hang on a minute, where exactly is it you are going?" she asked.

"Out with Jacey," I answered.

"Out where?"

"Urgh! Just out, Mum."

"I'm not sure about this," she said, then did what she always did whenever she wasn't sure about a situation involving me – called my Dad. "Gerald!"

Not being funny, but any time there is a situation that requires any kind of parenting, strictness, or authority, she immediately calls my dad. It's like she knows I will ignore any of the bullshit that comes out her mouth. She is an inept parent who can't even control her daughter; I mean, seriously, what's that about?

And she can't control me; that's the thing. I would ignore everything she says. I mean, honestly. What's she going to do? Lecture me to death?

She can go ahead and *bite me*.

So what does she have to do? Call on Dad. Because she can't exert any control without someone who owns a dick next to her. And I'm meant to look up to her? What a joke.

"What is it?" asks my dad, his slippers making that typical scuffling noise across the carpet. Mum tells him to pick his feet up as he walks and he dismisses her like everyone else does because she's a pathetic gutless moron who's not worth listening to.

"Honestly, dear, you can hear you coming a mile off." Then she turned her attention to me as I stood there poised with my hand on the door handle, ready to go and get wasted with my friends – you know, like proper teenagers do. "Did you know anything about Maya going out with Jacey?"

"No, I didn't. What is this?"

What is this?

It's like my dad's catchphrase. It doesn't even make sense. *What is this?* The more prevalent question would be: "Where?" or "Why?" or "When?" or "For how long?" Not "What is this?" It's illogical.

DICKS.

"What's what, Dad?"

"This? You're very dressed up. Are you going to see some boys?"

There is nothing more embarrassing than a man in his mid-fifties with an accent more middle-class than all of my teachers and tutors combined saying "boys." They aren't *boys*. They are *playthings*. And I want to *play*.

"I dunno, there might be some there, she didn't say."

I'm the best liar.

"I don't believe you."

Or not.

"Yes, I'm not too sure about this, Gerald," pipes up Mum. Way to go, Miss Feminist 2018 – you go and give your opinion to the man, who will ultimately make the final decision. Jesus, and you're meant to be my feminine role model? You couldn't even find your way out of a paper bag unless it had a shopping list in it.

"I agree," says the almighty man of the house. "I think you can stay in tonight. Have tea with us. Come on."

"No, I can't do that!" I say, hearing my voice go all high and hysterical, but they have to understand, they have to know how majorly PISSED OFF they make me. "I already promised Jacey!"

"Then you can un-promise her."

That makes no sense! Un-promise? It's not even a word! Look it up in the dictionary and I bet a hundred pounds it would not be there! This man is full of shit!

"No, I can't. I said I was—"

"You are staying home and that's final. Now come sit at the dinner table."

I throw my purse on the floor.

Stomp my foot.

Punch my fists into the air beside my waist.

"No! I don't want to have tea with you! You can do one! I hate you!"

Still, I never swear at them. Why? They are just my parents. Just two sad pathetic lonely people in a failing marriage because my dad has a wilting cock and my mum is as dry as a desert. Why don't I just tell them to fuck off? Why do I obey them? Why don't I just tell them to go suck my dick?

I could say that. Defy them. Tell them no.

Instead, I charge upstairs.

Well, I may not be able to swear at them or go against their ridiculous rules, but if they think they are having me sat at that tea table with them after this then they can think again. I never want to have tea with them again.

I never want to see them again.
DICKS.
I hope they die.
I hope I die.
I hope everyone dies.
I hate them!

❦ 7 ❦

THE ONE WHO DOESN'T BELONG

I f you had a bird in one hand and a rock in the other – what would you do?

I suppose most people's answer would be that they'd release the bird and throw the rock on the ground. Logical to some extent, I imagine.

But aren't you tempted to find out what happens if you didn't let the bird fly away? If you didn't throw the rock on the ground?

What would happen if you smashed your hands together, repeatedly, until that chirping little monster is nothing but bloody smush squashed against your palm?

It's like that feeling some people get. When you stand at the top of the hill, you look down, and you think – "I could jump."

You have no inclination to die, nor any suicidal tendencies, it's just a wild voice in your head telling you that it is a possibility. The voice of curiosity.

When you are driving, and a car comes toward you, and you think – "I could crash into that car. All it would take is a little swerve, and we would go head-on."

Half of you will say you have no idea what I'm talking about and think I'm weird.

The rest of you know what I mean.

Thing is, that little bit of curiosity, that morbid fascination of what could happen should you make these decisions you reject, that is what drives me.

I can't not investigate that curiosity.

I can't deny it. I pursue it. I love it; it's what makes me tick, what makes me keep getting out of bed in the morning.

I would smash my hands together again and again, ignoring the squelching, ignoring the manic chirps, ignoring the thick gunk spreading between my fingers – and I see how much the bird crumples and contorts.

I would jump off that hill and see how many rolls it takes to damage me.

I would swerve into that car and embrace the fire and embrace the pain and feel myself soar away from life as I entertain death.

That is why we are here. The five of us.

So far we've looked at the backstories of a black boxer and a petulant teenager. And there are three more to pick apart yet.

So.

What do you reckon?

Which one am I?

You have a one in five chance of getting it right.

Don't discount anyone until you've heard their stories. They – I mean *we* – are all horrible people.

Everyone in that room is the kind of person who would smash the bird against the rock.

Like you.

They just don't admit it.

I see you.

Reading my story like you're better than me.

Why don't you do something with your life?

❦ 8 ❦

1 HOUR 32 MINUTES

No one spoke, but everyone stared. Few of them had seen a dead body before and, even though this body seemed at peace, it's an experience that one does not adjust to lightly. Many seasoned police officers or army personnel may be numb to the sight of a corpse after years of experience – but I guarantee that every one of them was not so numb when faced with their first. Simply the concept of seeing a body void of life in itself is enough to make your stomach queasy and your throat dry up, but being stuck in a room with a body without a pulse, unable to escape the constant omen of your fate, can make your heart burst against your rib cage and your lungs wheeze under the strain of your heavy anxiety.

Milo is the exception to this, of course.

He's seen many dead bodies. Even made a few, too.

Ashley glances at his watch.

"Guys, we have less than half an hour now," he says.

No one responds.

Everly stares. Tariq stares. Even Ashley, as he states the fact that should make them all hurry into pertinent suggestions as to who amongst them the killer may be, still stares.

Milo lifts his head back and closes his eyes. Grins to himself. If he's going to go, then he's going to go. He's had plenty of dinners with death before; if he was a cat, his nine lives would have run out years ago.

"You lot," he sneers in a low growl, "are a bunch of bloody pussies."

Their heads slowly turn in Milo's direction.

"You know what?" Ashley says. "We have to figure out who the killer is to avoid the next person dying. And out of all of us – you're the one who seems to care nothing for this girl's death."

"Oh, cry me a river. First," he begins, still not moving from his relaxed position, "if I was the killer, I wouldn't make it this obvious, now would I? Second, I seen plenty of dead girls. And that bitch did my bloody head in."

Those words hung on the air like a potent odour: *I seen plenty of dead girls.*

Instantly, questions fired along the synapses of their brain cells, firing so many crucial interrogatives back and forth that they struggle to choose a question more pressing than the others.

Plenty of dead girls?

Where? Who? Why? When? Did you do it? Why did you do it? How had they been killed? Did you do that? When plenty?

But no questions come out of anyone's lips until the question is no longer a potent odour, but a vile stench of decay consuming the room.

"What are you?" Tariq eventually blurts out, still retaining a warily timid composure. "A serial killer?"

Milo snorts a laughter full of snot.

"No. A vet."

"What, with animals?" Everly asks, confused.

"A veteran, you stupid bitch."

"Oh."

Milo finally opens his eyes and moves them between the various eyes focussed on him, before settling on Ashley's. As he studies Ashley's face, really studies him, a flicker of recognition surfaces.

"I know you," Milo says.

"No, you don't."

"Not personally, but yeah, I know you. You're that boxer who won the silver at the Olympics."

"Yeah, that's me."

"Hah!" Milo projects a large, grumbly, ironic snort, followed by a laugh that would rival the most disgusting of hyenas.

"What's so funny?"

"All I'm sayin' is that your feet moved pretty nimble-like in that ring. You sure you ain't got no help or nothin'?"

"Fuck you, man," Ashley says, reacting in a way that he hopes will convince himself as much as Milo. He's been lying for so long now he's started to believe the lie.

"And I recognise you," Tariq says, directed at Milo.

"Oh yeah? I don't remember ordering no curry or nothing."

"Very funny. But, well, you would say that, wouldn't you?"

Milo stands.

"What the fuck you sayin'?" he asks, towering over Tariq. Even though he is in his sixties, Milo still has an impressive physique. His vest reveals two heavily tattooed arms – with some tattoos that Tariq would feel inclined to be offended by.

"Nothing," Tariq says, backing down.

Milo looks from Ashley to Tariq. "Well I ain't goin' to be made to stand here and get lectured by no paki and nigger."

"What did you just say?" Ashley demands, bursting forward, his body hunched over with a posture full of aggression. Tariq remains where he is, looking away so as to avoid confrontation.

"You heard me," Milo says, standing his ground as Ashley's expression morphs into an aggressive snarl.

"Yeah, well maybe you want to repeat it again, big man."

"Guys!" Evelyn interrupts. "Seriously, we have, like, no time, and we're going to die. Are we really doing this?"

Milo stands firm. Ashley backs off.

"Fine, whatever," Ashley says. "I think it's this guy." He points at Milo.

Milo chuckles sarcastically, as if he's just heard the stupidest, most ridiculous suggestion that has ever graced his ageing ears.

"I think I agree," Tariq admits.

"So if we decide it's him, how are we supposed to know if we're right?" Everly asks.

"Hey!" Ashley shouts out, turning around, aimed at no one in particular. "I think it's this guy! We all do!"

Nothing.

"I don't understand," Tariq says. "How do we know if we're correct?"

"What time you got there, Ashley ma boy?" Milo asks.

"We got twenty-two minutes, why?"

"Well, in answer to my Indian fellow over here–"

"I'm Bangladeshi."

"–I would predict that we'll find out if you're correct in twenty-two minutes, when we see if someone else snuffs it or not."

As they allow Milo's conclusion to simmer, their eyes shoot between each other's contraptions, the red lights attached to their bodies, wondering who would be next should they be wrong.

Although Ashley is pretty sure that they aren't.

9

MILO

A strong, southerly wind flutters what little grey hair I have left in its menacing bustle. A storm is on the way, I can feel it. My bones always get a little rigid when it's on its way. That's the thing with getting older, your bones ache, but they feel it more in bad weather – so much so you can tell when it's coming.

The weatherman said it was called Storm Azizah.

Jesus Fucking Christ.

Even the storms are getting immigrant names now.

I allow the rain to fire in my path. I see people, mostly young people, scuttling out the way, seeking shelter in a nearby shop, desperately huddling together under an umbrella.

Please.

I've been bombarded by all kind of weather, it doesn't scare me. In the Falklands, rain was the least of my worries. Bullets never sent me running, never mind a little drizzle. If anything, I like it. I embrace the chaos. The harsh sting of pelts of water. As it hits my skin I crave it to turn to hail so I can really feel it. Feel it dig harder. Feel it so my rough, coarse skin can feel something.

He sits before me. Where he always sits. Six years now, and not a Sunday goes by without me visiting. It still gets me every time.

Reduces an old man to tears.

Annie used to come with me. Back in the beginning. Then she decided she didn't want to anymore. That she couldn't. It was too tough.

But I kept going.

That's when she fucked off with a guy named Paul.

I broke his leg in two places, and he was too scared to tell anyone the truth.

Now I come here alone. Leave the pub shut for the morning. The drunks can go elsewhere. This is my day. Mine and Kyle's day. Kyle, the brave soldier.

That's what it reads on the tombstone.

Kyle Clunk
1991-2012
Her Majesty's Army
Beloved son and valiant soldier

He fought them. Died doing it.

Now they have invaded this country and no one seems to notice.

He goes to Iraq to kill them, they kill him, now they walk down our streets. In some cities, they even outnumber us. Seems like there's not a job a white British male can do that they can't rob.

Our off licenses. Our doctors. Our pharmacies. Our hospitals. Every sodding corner with every sodding curry house and sodding kebab shop, it makes me sick, it makes me rage – *fuck them all.*

Fuck them all back to where they came from.

They are fleeing their country because it's too dangerous over there?

Weren't too dangerous to make my son run away, was it?

He went over there, to this supposedly dangerous place. He went over there, didn't he?

To save your fucking country.

Now you come over here.

If it was good enough for my son to die in, it's good enough for them to rot in.

Now this is modern Britain. Modern England. Where you dislike the invasion of these fucking Arabs and that makes me racist, because I want our country to belong to our country.

My fucking son died for this country.

And it's been invaded. Just not with weapons.

Who's going to save this country now, eh? Who?

I try, but it can't be me alone. It has to be *us*. You. Me. The rest of my mates. We protest in towns that have been hit most. And we make sure our voices are heard. Make sure that our sons aren't dying in vain. That no sharia law will be passed in my country.

Over my dead body.

Over my dead fuckin' corpse, rotting in the ground beneath their fucking curry houses and *stinky curry fucking fingers.*

FUCK THEM.

I get myself so riled when I visit Kyle. I get myself livid, my gut twists, it churns, my thoughts get infected, it's like a virus, like a plague running through me. This hate. This defiance. This refusal to accept it.

I need to stop getting so angry.

I close my eyes.

Cool myself down.

I must stop getting so worked up about it. Getting worked up will do nothing to change nothing. It'll do nowt but give me a heart attack. The doctor – a fucking English one, like I remember they used to be – told me I got to watch my ticker. Got to make sure it stays healthy.

For the sake of my life.

For the sake of saving myself from immigrant surgeons.

Last thing I need is for one of them to be sticking their grubby fucking curry hands into my chest. I'd rather have a clean corpse, thank you.

Rather be left out in this rain to wash myself clean. Rather die than be touched by them. Rather be buried next to my son.

My son, who died for *you*.

For *you*.

And you judge me! You cannot judge me until your child is brought home in a coffin because a bunch of liberal dicks allow them into this once-great country.

This...

Once-great...

I bow my head. I'm doing it again. Getting angry. I need to be sorrowful. Need to think about my brave, beloved son, not the shit-stain of a country we're in.

I'm sorry, Kyle.

Sorry this country had to do this to you.

Sorry you had to pay the price for them.

For *them*.

Sorry it seems to be for nothing.

I stand. Walk away. Don't look back. I spend my five minutes with him, but I never look back. I can't. Otherwise, I'll never leave.

Before I reach the exit to the graveyard, my left arm begins to tingle. I don't know what's happening, but one minute it's tickling, the next I'm choking on my own breath.

I drop to the floor.

It has to happen now, doesn't it?

Just as I was thinking about—

A searing pain in my chest interrupts my thought.

It's as if I can feel my heart slow down and stop. No longer thudding against my chest. No longer pumping my British blood around my body.

Well, fuck it, if I'm going out in a graveyard, then it seems well suited.

My heart is stopping next to Kyle.

I'm coming, son.

Fuck this.

Fuck them.

10

1 HOUR, 38 MINUTES

"So what do we do now?" Milo muses, leaning against the wall. "You all made your decision. You all seem to think it's me. We got a little bit of time to kill. What say we all hold hands and sing kum-by-fucking-yah?"

Tariq turns his head away and flinches.

"What's the matter, Banglaboy? Offended by my filthy mouth?"

"Among other things, yes."

"Oh yeah? What other things are they?"

Tariq shakes his head.

"Come on, browny, let's have it."

"Browny?" Tariq retorts. "All the racist words in the world, and you have to come up with browny?"

Tariq shakes his head, peering venom into his fascist opposition. His body recoils into itself, turned away from Milo, shielding his painful expression with his shoulder. He would love to claw at Milo's face, punch him, maybe even kick him – but that is not the kind of person he is. He is the kind of person who gives the school bully his lunch before he has to be told. He's the kind of person who apologises for things he didn't do to make his wife stop being mad at him. He's the kind of person who allows his kids to fight because he'd rather pretend they all secretly get along.

Tariq has never been in a confrontation in his life that he hasn't immediately evaded.

So he'd love to stand up to Milo. Love to make him shut his grimy mouth.

But he won't.

Because he doesn't have it in him.

He's the kind of person who pays other people to fight his battles for him.

And at that thought, a creepy realisation boils the base of his gut. He knows Milo. Personally knows him. Although Milo doesn't personally know Tariq.

He bows his head. He realises there is a reason that he and Milo have been picked together.

"Come on, I'm waiting. Don't like being called browny, what else can I call you, eh? Paki?"

"I'm not a Paki."

"Oh, ain't you?"

"I'm from Bangladesh," he replies. He wishes he'd added more to his response, such as, "You fool," or, "You idiot," but his fears for where this conflict could go cripple his disposition. He fears doing more to aggravate this man than simply pointing out his mistaken heritage.

"Is that so?" Milo taunts. "It's all the same, ain't it? India, Pakistan, Bangladeshi. Abu-fucking-Dhabi – it's all the same. They shit all over their women and steal our jobs."

Tariq goes to reply.

His mouth opens, a witty response on the tip of his lips.

It hovers there, breathing across his tongue, ready to be released.

But that's where it remains. In his mouth. In his thoughts. Because he's not the kind of man to stand up for his own rights.

He's not any kind of man, really. And that's how he feels in that moment – not worthy of the title 'man.' Not even able to defend his heritage or his history. Sad. Pathetic. Again.

"Come on!" Milo prompts.

"I don't want to get into it," Tariq says.

"Don't want to get into it? Come on. We gots all day."

Ashley checks his watch.

Actually, no they don't.

❧ 11 ❧
MILO

I wake up in a room surrounded by brown people. Brown people with surgical masks. Standing over me. Celebrating. Thrilled.

They beat death. I'm awake.

One of them stays and tells me I'm lucky to have survived, though I can barely understand him.

"Speak English," I tell him.

"I speak English very well, thank you very much," he says in a pathetic excuse for the language *we* invented. "And if you please, I will be telling you about what happened."

"Okay, sunshine. What happened?"

He continues to tell me that I had a heart attack. That I'm lucky to be alive. That he saved me.

That *he* saved me.

That I'm alive because of *him*.

And suddenly I don't know what to think. What to feel.

Maybe if we had a British doctor taking care of me I wouldn't have ended up having a heart attack in the first place. Would have had a better course of treatment. They'd have given me pills sooner. Prevented it.

But I know I'm lying to myself.

"Do you have any other questions so far?" he asks me.

Yeah.

A few.

How do you look yourself in the mirror, you dirty prick?

You killed my son.

You killed my son.

You *killed* my *son*.

I shake my head. No questions.

He gives me a prescription. Tells me to take these pills. Tells me I need them to stay alive. That without them, the same thing would just happen again.

And I'd end up back here.

I don't want to end up back here.

I don't want to ever see him again.

He saved me.

He saved *me*.

But at what cost?

Filthy-fucking-Muslim-piece-of-shit.

Who saved my life.

That filthy-fucking-Muslim-piece-of-shit saved my life.

"This is the last you will be seeing of me, I hope," he says as I continually endeavour to decipher his accent. "Remember to take the pills, and I hope you have a nice day."

You hope I have a nice day?

I just had a heart attack, you moron.

"Hey, Doc," I say, just as he removes his gloves and goes to leave the room.

"Yes?"

"Where'd you come from?"

"Birmingham. I live in Birmingham."

"No, I mean before that, before you came to Birmingham. Where you from?"

He looks at me with confusion. As if trying to figure out

what my motivation is, as if this is some kind of trick. As if this is some kind of trap I'm setting him up for.

"My family comes from India, if that is what you're saying. We moved here twenty years ago. My daughter and my son are British."

I shake my feeble head.

Come off it.

Your kids ain't British.

They will *never* be British.

Why's he even telling me all this? Why do I care about his kids?

Why do I care about his ridiculous, cheap, pathetic words?

"And who in India gave you your doctorship?" I ask, scrutinising his face.

"Actually, I came over here to study medicine at university, then went on to do my masters and my PhD whilst studying here."

"Here?" I bark. "Where?"

"In Birmingham. Why do you ask?"

He studied here. A product of the British education system. Taking a place in our education system that would have undoubtedly been given to a minority, just because they are a minority. So they can tick that box.

He watches me. Waits for an explanation.

"I was just wondering, Doc."

"Keep well, Mr Clunk," he says as he leaves.

And I'm alive.

Because of him.

I'm alive because of him.

I say it to myself but I don't believe it.

I'm alive because of him. The man from India who lives in Birmingham.

Is India anywhere near Iraq anyway?

1 HOUR, 48 MINUTES

A sparkling silver reflection flickers from behind Milo's foot.

In a brief respite between relentless panic and hopeless fear, the item draws Everly's attention. She stares at it with such dumfounded shock that she can't quite understand why it roused her so.

"What's that?" she asks, her voice small and weary.

"Wha'?" Milo grunts, his pruned face displaying further disdain with an obnoxious curling of his nose.

"What is that?" Everly demands with more conviction, her finger pointing at the shiny surface behind the piece of bony fat Milo recognises as his thigh.

With a narrowing of his already narrowed eyes, he lifts his leg and reveals the item in all its glory.

"A door handle!" Ashley declares, his voice intense, but his exhausted body drained of adrenaline.

Milo nonchalantly raises the item to his face and inspects each surface with unneeded scrutiny, surveying the shape with such a prolonged, feigned interest that it infuriates the others awaiting a verdict.

"Oh yeah," he says, feeling its weight in a small bounce.

Ashley abruptly recollects the hole in the wall behind him, and he turns to inspect it again. The hole is a small cylinder that would fit perfectly the small, elongated strip of metal attached to the door handle. A surge of hope lifts him, optimistic glances shared with the others.

A door. They found a door. And the door handle.

"Quick, give it here," Ashley prompts, reaching out his hand and prompting Milo with a slight wave of his fingers.

"Excuse me?" Milo gloats.

"Give me the door handle!"

"You didn't say please," grins Milo, ever the obtuse prick.

Ashley's hope combines with a manic rush of rage. It tickles his veins from his shoulder to his fingers, from his groin to his toes; from the highest strand of hair on his head to the multitude of muscles clenching and shaking throughout his body.

"Are you fucking kidding me?" Ashley cries.

"You're an idiot."

Ashley's cheeks redden. His fists clench. He shakes with a diseased violence – unable to focus his livid body into staying still.

"Do you really think" – Milo begins, the way someone who's gained age without gaining wisdom might begin in their typically deluded manner – "that the one who put is in here would really make it that easy?"

Ashley leaps forward, his well-trained arm retracted in readiness, his mouth curled into a twisted snarl of fury. But, just as his leap takes him toward Milo, the restraint around his ankle holds him in place – wrenching him back at the last moment, Milo's dormant, unaltered body sits mere inches from Ashley's desperately anguished fists.

Milo's entire body jolts in guffaws, toppling over in a rolling riot, kicking and cackling in a way that makes Ashley's sweaty fists all the more eager.

"I will kill you," Ashley barks. "I swear, I will kill you!"

Ashley's eyes turn to Tariq, who, too timid to engage with the type of rage Ashley might, turns to Everly, childish vulnerability painted on his face.

"Just give him the door handle," says Everly.

"Fine," Milo agrees between continuous snorts of laughter that show little sign of slowing down. "Here, have it."

Milo throws the door handle at Ashley with more thrust than is needed.

Ashley lifts it, clumsily clambering it between his fumbling fingers in his eagerness to escape. He aligns it with the hole in the wall, slots it in perfectly, and looks to the others.

It fits.

He presses down on the door and...

No.

He tries again, putting all his weight down upon it, and...

No.

Maybe he's just not doing it right. Door handles can be fiddly. He remembers how his grandma's door handle always used to jar, meaning you had to lift the door with it for it to open.

He tries lifting the door handle instead.

It doesn't budge.

He pushes the door handle further into the hole, pressing downwards, then upwards.

He pulls it out slightly, making it looser, lifting it up, then pressing it down.

He tries every combination and every attempt and every option and every idea there is that involves using a door handle, but none of them work.

It's locked.

Milo's fit of laughter returns.

Ashley retracts the handle with the speed of an athlete and uses all his muscle to launch it at Milo.

Milo, too busy in hysterics to notice, feels the door handle land against the centre of his forehead with enough force to not only shut up him, but to make him yelp in pain.

"It's you!" Ashley claims. "I know it is!"

Milo lifts his head, blood drooling from an open gash slightly above his eyebrows. He blinks it out of his eyes, wipes it from obscuring his vision, feels it cascade down his cheeks, tasting it on his lips.

"You fucking black prick," he says. "Violent, the lot of you. All the same."

"You say another thing about me being black," Ashley says, remonstrating with his finger, "I'll find something else to throw, and I'll aim it at your throat."

They all look away from each other.

And, given the temporary relief from prying eyes, the one who does not belong grins.

But only for a moment.

Not long to go now.

The second death is soon.

❧ 13 ❧

TARIQ

I t's the same old story.

I am scum. Foreign trash. Pollution. Vermin. A dirty migrant. I do not belong here. I'm a leech on your society. I'm a disgusting immigrant invading your way of life. I'm this, I'm that, I'm something, I'm nothing – but whatever it is I am, I do not deserve the same rights as you do.

At least that's what the idiot who put the brick through my pharmacy window thought.

The third brick in the space of a few months.

But everyone says the same thing. "Good job you have insurance." "It's just a brick." "Don't take it personally."

It's just a brick? Not personal?

Shut up, you fools.

I'm sorry for being so forthright.

But then again, I'm not.

What do you want me to tell you? A lie? An alternate reality?

If you were looking for a new story, full of original ideas and twists and turns that haven't happened before, then I am sorry, but my segment of the story is not for you. Go read *Gone Girl*, or *Girl on the Train*, I hear those books are hugely original. Riveting, even. Will keep you turning the pages for hours. And, luckily for you, they don't leave you having to face the reality of what hardworking people deal with day-to-day in *your* society.

But if you were looking for the truth, then read on. If you wish to witness the looks, the comments, the judgements that show the subtle fascism underlying this country, then you're in for a treat. If you wanted to read about what British society seems to deem as something I just need to 'accept' – then you are in for the read of your life.

I don't even understand why you hate me. Because of terrorists? Because someone committed a horrible act, and you think because I share their skin colour and religion that means I share their values? That it makes me dangerous? Well, by that logic, maybe I should judge all white British people as dangerous because of the minority that spit on me in the street and tell me to go back to my own country.

I hold the brick in my hand.

"Just a brick," they say.

No, it's not just a brick. It will never be *just* a brick.

The police come around again, but there's no point. They say the same thing as last time, and the time before.

"We'll file a report."

"Let us know if you see anything suspicious."

"Not really much we can do."

I don't understand that. They don't do anything – they don't look for prints on the brick, they don't look at traffic cameras, they don't even bother looking at my CCTV because they know whoever did this has their hood up and their scarf around their face.

I understand the police are underfunded and under-resourced.

I'm sure that's why they are so reluctant to do any of the things I suggest.

Their money has to go on murders and rapes and drug busts – not on some business owner facing repeated racial attacks.

I'm sure that's what it is.

And I am completely sure it's nothing to do with the fact that I'm not deemed part of their society because my birth certificate does not read *United Kingdom*.

I don't even watch them as their police car speeds away this time. I no longer have the hope that this will change, that they will act, that there is something they will do that will stop this.

Instead, I stand behind the counter – not the main counter, but behind the small wall where all the drugs and prescriptions are kept. I stand there surrounded by the medicines that would not be supplied to people in need if it weren't for me owning this business. Giving it to people who'd rather I wasn't here.

I know not everyone feels this way. In fact, I am sure of it. But it seems that everyone who walks in looks at me with a flicker in their eye, a brief moment in their first recognition of me, that identifies that I am not one of them. They probably don't even realise it on a conscious level – but somewhere in there, in the back of their mind, a fleeting thought of recognition passes saying, "He's a Muslim." Or, "He's brown." "He's Indian." "He's Bangladeshi."

Or, as the note that was wrapped around my brick in my hand reads: *Fuck of home paki.*

The most offensive thing about it is that they can't even spell *off* right, and they claim it's their language.

But I do what I did the same time last month when the last message came through my window.

I contact the insurance company, who now know me by name, then just get on with it. Continue running my business like nothing happened.

Because – what else am I going to do?

I have a wife. Two glorious children that I praise Allah for every day. A business that I own and run. I have made a good home for me here.

And I like it.

And I'm going to keep it.

I fill a few more bags with a few more boxes of pills. I call out their names and they collect them. Most of them smile. Say thank you. Do so without contempt.

This place isn't so bad.

Strange, how these strangers realise so little about what that simple thank you does for me.

Then *he* enters.

He's not young, that's for sure. His skin has wrinkled and faded in the way that it only does with years of alcohol and tobacco. Even so, his chest has more muscle than he should be afforded, and he walks with a limp that only comes from hard times. His arms are covered in tattoos, most of them faded, but among them are clear symbols of who he is. Nothing as bold as a swastika – but images that hint at where he stands. A St. George's flag alone would not label one a racist, I understand that, but when accompanied by the Celtic Cross, SS bolts, and the words *blood and honour* in Bloodhound font, his political ideologies are made apparent to anyone who looks at him for more than a few seconds.

His eyes meet mine for a very brief moment, but I can feel it. His sneer. His hatred. His contempt.

But there's something else in his eyes.

Something deeper. Something that terrifies me. Something that tells me I need to be scared of this man, of what he has done, and of what he can do.

One of the young ladies who works for me serves him. Takes his prescription and passes it to me. Benazepril. Enalapril. Moexipril. All parts of a treatment for the heart, possibly following a cardiac arrest.

I look at the man.

He leans on the counter. Out of breath. Shaking his head.

I fill out his prescription and read the name out.

"Milo Clunk."

At first his eyes close. He waits a second. As if considering whether to be aggressive, dismissive, or just darn rude.

"Milo Clunk," I repeat, looking straight at him.

"Here," he finally grunts.

I hand the bag to him. He snatches it away from me and staggers out, limping and clutching his chest.

As he walks out he lingers by the smashed window. He looks back at me. Then to the smashed window. Then back at me.

As if to gloat.

As if to show off.

As if to take pride in his work.

❧ 14 ☙

1 HOUR, 56 MINUTES

"Guys," Everly says. "What if it's not Milo?"

Milo snorts another snotty laugh.

"You think 'bout this now?" he says between sniggers. He feels for his pocket, as if reaching for a cigarette, then finds there is none there.

"We've made our decision," Ashley confirms. "We have to stick with it."

"Well, I can tell you," Milo continues in his arrogant matter-of-fact fashion, "One of you is going to die in a few minutes. 'Cause it ain't me."

"You tell us this now?" Tariq says.

"Oh, look who's piping up."

"What is your problem with me, man?"

"Man? What you trying to talk like?"

"Shut up!" Ashley shouts, fed up, aggravated by useless conflict. "Just – shut up! Whatever your beef is, man, just leave it. We got shit to sort out."

Milo shrugs his shoulders nonchalantly and leans his head back. He sighs a long, exasperated sigh, as if he were breathing

61

out a large drag of his absent cigarette, but instead breathes any worries he had left in him. There is nothing on his face that shows even a slight concern about imminent death.

"So you are swearing it, ain't you?" Ashley asks.

"Does it matter? I could have sworn all the past hour, sworn 'til I was blue in the bloody face. You've made up your mind."

Ashley looks to Tariq. To Everly. To his watch.

Three minutes.

They still have time to change their mind.

Then again, maybe that's what Milo wants.

"What do we think, guys?" Ashley asks, terror spread over his face.

He doesn't want to die.

The ticking clock reminds him of the inevitability.

He could be next.

"What do you mean, what do we think?" Everly replies.

"Do we want to change our mind?"

"To who? One of us?"

"I don't know."

"Maybe it's you."

"Well it ain't."

"Yeah, but I could tell you that, and he could tell you that, even this arsehole" – she points at Milo – "could tell you it isn't him. We are all going to say that. But it is one of us. Isn't it?"

"Unless it isn't."

"What?"

"Maybe it's a trick. What if we all, together, decide it's none of us? Maybe that's the real answer."

"No," Tariq decides. "We must stick with our decision. Now's not a time to falter. We have decided him, let's stay him."

"You just got it in for me, don't you?" Milo says.

"As a matter of fact–"

"Fucking quit it!" Ashley repeats.

He turns around. Faces the wall. Arms on the back of his head. Breathing heavily. Head full of mess.

He can't look at them anymore.

He looks at his watch instead, then wishes he hadn't.

He straightens his chest. Does some breathing exercises. Stretches his body out. All things his coach had told him to do when he was feeling anxious.

Anxious?

Hah!

Anxious is a mild adjective for what he's feeling.

His mind races with a hundred thoughts, each one worse than the one before it. He changes his mind multiple times, questioning their decision, then questioning it again.

He turns toward the others, but his eyes don't acknowledge them. Instead, he sees his mum's face. His proud, doting, delusional mother. She did everything for him, and where is she now? Somewhere alone.

Does she even know he's gone?

Has he even been reported as a missing person yet?

Have they gone looking in his flat and found his needles?

He can see the headlines tomorrow. *Disgraced former Olympian goes missing amid steroid controversy.*

And he can see his mother's face as she cries over his wall, not knowing what to think. But still proud. Still the solid rock she's always been.

"Ashley," Everly says in a panicked voice poorly disguised as calm. "What's our decision?"

Ashley turns back to Tariq. To Everly. To Milo.

"We stick with our decision."

He turns back to the wall. Leans his head against the rusty surface. Feels its steely toughness cement against his head.

This is the biggest fight of his life.

And he doesn't have any needles to help him with this one.

He doesn't need to look at his watch to know that they have one minute left.

What if this is his final minute?

What if it's Tariq or Everly that dies next, and he's stuck with Milo?

Jesus, now I'm deciding who I want to die least...

His eyes flutter to Maya's dead body.

The sight stings him with the pertinent realisation of impossible truth, of certain, inescapable avoidance. The appearance of what happens once the hour is up.

It's a harsh reality, but being in such close proximity to death is something a human can adjust to far more easily than one could imagine. Nearly two hours stuck alone with a corpse and they no longer notice it, like it's furniture, or paint drying on a wall – once applied, it is permanently there but never acknowledged.

But your own death – you will deny its possibility until there's no breath left to deny. This isn't like in a boxing ring. It is barely a game. In the ring it's a fair fight. In the past two hours alone, he'd taken more shots below the belt than a referee would allow.

A quiet beeping begins, faintly in the background.

The first thing Ashley does is check his head. Then his torso. Then his legs. Then every part of his body. Searching to see if it is him that is beeping, even though he's searched himself multiple times and found nothing on him.

He turns around to find that Tariq and Everly have done the same thing.

All eyes turn to Milo.

A small spot of flashing red light reflects in the wall behind the base of his skull.

They were wrong.

It wasn't him.

Which means it was one of them.

Ashley knows it isn't him.

But so does Everly. So does Tariq.

They all know.

But it has to be someone.

It has to be one of them.

Someone has to be lying.

Unless it's a trick.

Unless one of the other two want me to think it's a trick.

He looks at Maya. *Maybe she's faking it.* In a horror movie it would definitely be Maya. The typical, predictable twist; she suddenly stands up and reveals herself.

But they felt her pulse. Her body was rigid. She was dead. And Milo is about to join her.

Three left.

Ashley does not want to face the truth, but he knows he must – *it is one of them.*

Milo uses the wall to steady himself as he stands. The others back off, but he raises a hand and waves it as if to say they needn't fear, he has no intention of forcing his death upon anyone else.

Milo looks to the terrified faces of the others. Terrified, yes, but he has no doubt they were all secretly doing leaps for joy that they get to live at least another hour.

"Well," Milo declares, "ain't this ironic?"

The ticking ends and the base of his skull explodes. A large lump of flesh splatters the wall behind him, followed by pieces of scalp, brain, and skin, smacking against the wall, leaving a bloody trail as they drip downwards.

Tariq wretches as Milo's headless body flops to the ground.

Everly turns and covers her face, weeping without control.

Ashley stares at the open neck, twisted and contorted, and inside out in so many ways.

He pricks with morbid fascination.

Then he realises it's real.

He grows horrified – not because of the sight, as unappealing as it is, but because of what this now means.

He'd already realised it, but now its unmistakeable clarity punches him in the gut with a sickening strike.

It isn't Milo.

15

MILO

I wish it was me.

I'm not talking about the one who doesn't belong – I couldn't give less of a shit who doesn't belong, or who dies in that room of sodding losers.

I'm talking about the smashed window in the pharmacy.

I wish that it was me who had done it. I'd have loved to have seen the look on his scrawny little face when he discovered the window and the perfectly articulated note that came with it.

The look of disgust, of pure distasteful horror, as the extent of the offense he has taken slowly settles on his face. While it changes in slow motion.

I'd have loved to have put the last remaining strength I have in my right arm into a heave, a rugged throw, bursting the brick along the wind, listening to the satisfied smash of the glass breaking into a thousand individual pieces.

But it wasn't me.

Honest.

Why would I lie? I'd love to take credit for it. After all, this is just between you and me; Tariq ain't going to know.

But it wasn't me.

It didn't do it to the snivelling little ratbag.

My arm would probably fire out the socket if I attempted to throw a brick like that. It can barely manage to keep my cup of tea steady. It ain't what it was. Years of lifting heavy weapons have given me muscles of a weakling, meaning my shoulder stings like a bitch any time I try to lift anything. They'd laugh me out of the army now.

Yet, even as much as I would love to have been the one parading their patriotic beliefs in front of his business, as much as I would love to have seen the anger spread across that little Asian fucker's face, I...

I just...

I don't know, anymore.

What am I supposed to say?

Am I supposed to lie to myself?

To you?

Fuck that.

If I could have done it, I would have done it. But I don't think I could have.

And not just because of my lack of upper arm strength.

Although that creates a huge difficulty, yes – but just imagine, for a moment, that I do have use of my arm and I could do it.

Well, then...

I couldn't.

A week ago, yes. Give me the full use of this deteriorating body and I would be there with a whole pile of bricks, ready to launch a full-on assault.

Not now.

Not after one of them...

Saved.

Me.

I can't say it.
I can't even say it.

The racist is gone. Does anyone care?

It's time to paint him in a suit and talk about how great he was when he was alive, like you always do in your funeral of lies.

They always seem so great once they've gone.

✣ 16 ✣

2 HOURS, 5 MINUTES

T ense, turgid looks exchange between the final three captives. Looks that they attempt to disguise, but seep through like water through sand. Looks of doubt, of distrust, of wariness.

Milo's death was the curve ball the remaining survivors needed to evoke their suspicions.

They are all promptly aware that this may be the end of their lives, and with every hour, those chances get higher and the odds get worse.

They started at five to one.

Then four to one.

Now there's three.

Soon it will be fifty-fifty.

That is, if they survive the next hour.

Ashley.

Everly.

Tariq.

They know it has to be one of them.

Ashley decides to take charge. He stands, giving an air of

composure that he hasn't recognised in the others – a defiant, definite, decision-making mind taking over as he averts his eyes away from the corpses either side of his feet. But the moment he goes to speak with the decisive voice he has mentally coerced himself into, he looks at Everly and Tariq and he remembers – *it's one of them.*

Or so they were told.

He backs down.

Each of them find their bodies physically aching. Drowning in the fatigue of anxiety. A tired state mixed with an alert state can produce a headache that would rival any dirty hangover.

It is said that wrinkles are evidence of a good life lived – that they are evidence that one has experienced life to the full. This includes all the ups and downs, but I imagine that it's the downs that cause most of these wrinkles. And if that's the case, then they are ageing by the second.

And they are feeling it.

Feeling their muscles limpening, feeling their energy drain. The adrenaline is long gone now and all that is left is despair.

There was always that possibility in the background of their thoughts that this was fake. That this was staged. That they were somehow being pranked. That a television show presenter was going to burst in at any moment, laughing with the composure of a lunatic, pointing out where each camera was hidden

But that possibility is now deceased.

The pieces of skull and brain and skin and face and blood and puss and hair and violence that decorate the walls following Milo's demise is enough evidence for them to presume that the threat is not only strong, or that it is sickeningly pertinent – but that it is inevitable, and there is little they can do about it.

Ashley leaps to his feet and does what he should have done two hours ago.

He bashes every wall, stomps every bit of floor, leaps to

every inch of the ceiling. He attempts to barge open their confines, his thrashing echoing around the metallic box, his perseverance failing to wear thin. Multiple actions of pressing his ear to the wall assured him there is hollow space outside their containment, and he is determined to find his way out.

"It's no good," Everly weakly speaks.

"What?" Ashley retorts.

"It's no good. Whoever's got us in here has got us in here. There's no escape."

"Well at least I'm fuckin' doing something!" Ashley stands back and looks at the wall, then continues bashing against it. He has always been someone to take action; even at school, he'd get in trouble for standing up to teachers he thought were unfair. He despises people who are happy to just sit back and accept things as they are – his steroid abuse notwithstanding. "We've been playing this all wrong. It's trying to make us argue. What we need to do is find a way to escape from it."

"It?"

Ashley stops and realises he has been referring to their situation, and the villain who placed them in said predicament, as 'it.' Not he, or she – *it*. And this only highlights further to Ashley how little hope they have.

"Guys," says Tariq, squatting over Milo, taking something from the corpse's pocket.

It is a note, and as he reveals it, the other two gather over his shoulder.

"Why's it in his pocket?" Everly asks.

The question lingers like fog on the air.

"Maybe he put it there," Tariq suggests. "Or maybe whoever put us in here put it there."

"I'm pretty sure that wasn't there a few minutes ago," Ashley points out.

They look at each other sheepishly, exchanging looks of

suspicion. Each of them rack their minds to remember where the others had been in the last few minutes. Trying to decide who may have had an unnoticed opportunity to place a letter in the corpse of this racist imbecile.

And it doesn't escape Ashley's attention that Tariq is the one who discovered it.

"Both of you turn out your pockets," Ashley demands. He does it himself to prove that there are no further notes.

Tariq and Everly quickly follow. Nothing.

Ashley contemplates what to do next.

"Surely we should read the–" Tariq goes to say.

"No," Ashley interrupts, snatching the note and throwing it to the floor. "If one of us is planting notes on the others, then they have to have those notes somewhere."

"What do you suggest?" Everly asks.

Ashley hesitates. Sighs.

"We search each other."

"Okay," Tariq agrees, and holds his hands out.

"No. Patting down won't do it. We need to be thorough."

"How thorough?"

"We strip. Let the others look in our clothes. Show each other our bodies. Show we have nothing to hide."

"I'm not stripping off in front of you two," Everly objects, her eyes narrowing, both demeaned and degraded by the suggestion.

"It's not a sex thing, don't get excited. I don't give a shit what your tits look like." He pulls a face like Everly is the most ridiculous person in the world. "But if one of us is the killer, the easy way to know would be to check, right? Yeah?"

"Go to hell. I am not taking my clothes off in front of you."

She folds her arms, glaring at him with such intent she practically pierces a hole through his chest.

Ashley looks at his watch, then back up at her.

"We don't have time for this."

Her arms remain folded as her head turns away.

Ashley steps forward. Stands intimidatingly over her. He's a boxer, and he knows how to cast someone in a shadow that will make them feel small – but Everly stands tall. Ever the feminist.

"Maybe you protest too much," Ashley says in a slow, sinister voice.

"Maybe we need to–" Tariq attempts, but is ignored and interrupted.

"I'll go first," Ashley decides.

He takes his top off. He watches Everly out the corner of his eye, sure that she won't be able to help affording herself a glance before shifting her eyes away, repulsed at herself for doing so. His biceps are thick, his pecs are sculpted, and his abs are expertly moulded; he's used to women looking at him.

He removes his tracksuit bottoms next, leaving just his underwear. As he does this, he throws his top and trousers to the other two. Tariq inspects every part of the clothing, then hands it to Everly. With a look of preposterous redundancy, she takes the clothes and looks herself.

"You still have something on," she points out, then instantly regrets it.

This is the point Ashley would usually stop.

Steroids have a way of making some of you bigger, and some of you smaller.

But he is committed. His life is resting on the removal of his underwear and, as ridiculous as that thought makes him feel, he has to go through with it.

He removes his Calvin Klein boxers and throws them at the others. He turns his head away so he doesn't have to look at them, so he doesn't see the laughs, the giggles, the agape mouths in astonishment that something could be that small.

Fucking steroids, he thinks.

He puts his hands in the air and turns around, showing his round arse cheeks, and eventually returning to full frontal.

"Satisfied?" Ashley asks.

The others blankly nod.

"Right, give me my clothes back."

They throw his clothes back and he returns them to his shivering body.

"Right, Everly, we'll be kind. Tariq, you go next."

With a glance of shame to Everly, he bows his head. He has been married for most of his life and no new woman has seen him naked in a long time. He feels guilty, as if he is betraying his wife somehow – but also feels inadequate, like he doesn't want to be judged.

After all, how would you feel taking your clothes off in front of two strangers with two corpses at your feet and the pressing urgency of death lurking on the next hour?

Tariq shyly presents his torso, perfectly preserved as what magazines have come to know as 'the dad bod.' He throws his ill-fitting chinos to the others, along with his white briefs. They inspect, allow him to rotate, and return his clothes. He feels glad that their expression didn't falter, and that he needn't feel judged.

"Okay, honey," Ashley says, immediately regretting using the condescending term to address her, knowing this will inevitably make her less responsive. "It's time."

She folds her arms and gives him the look his mum used to give him when he arrived home drunk out of his face at fifteen. It is what she termed 'the stink eye', and he has come to know the expression well.

"You can give me that face all you want," he says. "If you ain't guilty, you'll do it."

"Or maybe if I'm not willing to be your stripper then I will die with some dignity."

"Come on," Tariq says in a voice barely audible. "Please."

She looks to Tariq and rolls her eyes, aggravated. Annoyed at everything. At Ashley for proposing the stupid idea, at Tariq for persuading her, and at herself for agreeing to undress before two blokes. She knows if the killer is her or not, she does not need to prove anything – except she does, and she knows this, deep down.

Her vest comes off first, getting caught in the steel contraption fixed around her neck, which only exasperates her temper further. She throws the vest at Ashley with the vigour of a baseball pitcher and the aggression of a UFC fighter. He takes it without breaking his face of steel and checks it.

Next, she removes her jeans and throws them at him. Scars from years of self–abuse glisten on the inside of her thigh – the necessity to hide them does not come up much to a single mother who works at the checkouts. Intimacy is something she is rarely afforded. She feels embarrassed, and guilty for feeling so. But it comes as a relief that the others don't seem to care.

She covers her bra with her arms.

"We still got a bit to go," Ashley points out.

"Really?" she says, shaking her head with a face full of spite.

"Come on, just get this over with."

With a scowl, she moves her arms to her back – which may have only been a small, insignificant movement, but still displays all the disgust and anger she is currently feeling – then she allows her bra to drop. Her underwear comes next, and she thought she could not feel worse than she did when she woke up in this room, but she can, and she does.

Ashley and Tariq are prompt in returning her clothes, and they all turn away and face the wall as she redresses.

An uncomfortable silence descends on the room. A feeling that they are truly lost.

No one had anything to hide. No more hidden notes.

But what did they expect?

For it to be that easy?

"What now then, genius?" Everly spits.

"I'm sorry," Ashley says without any sincerity. "We had to know."

"Well now you know. And I know you're a dick."

"Hey, I don't want to be here any more than you do."

"So what's the next move then, big shot?"

Ashley's mouth moves but no words are produced.

"How about we read the note?" Tariq suggests.

The note. Ashley had forgotten. He picks it up.

They each gather around him, as much as their chains allow them. Close enough to read, but far enough so as not to feel anyone's skin or breath upon their own.

Two down, three to go.

But I am still one of you.

You seem to be rather useless at this, so how about I give you a clue?

To figure out who I am, figure out who has less to hide.

Good luck.

Their eyes each rise and meet each other's.

"But we know none of us has anything to hide," Tariq says. "We just proved it."

"Perhaps it doesn't mean physically," Ashley says.

Everly huffs once more, folds her arms, turns around and walks waywardly to the other side of the room, stepping over Maya's leg like it was a twig in her path, or a toy her child had discarded on the living room floor.

"Okay, so let's try and figure this out," Ashley says. "Who are you?"

17

EVERLY

I sit on the same seat with the same numb arse cheeks with the same fake smile I wear every other same day.

It's not glamorous.

It never was.

But it pays the bills.

It doesn't pay them as well as it did when I...

Well...

At least I can preserve my integrity. That's what I tell myself. But when a customer comes up with a pack of bananas without a barcode and has a go at me for it – that's when I'd trade it all back in and go back to that life.

I have a child now.

A child without a father.

I'm not the Virgin Mary. Far from it. I'm just a woman with a past full of mistakes.

But he isn't one of them.

And he's why. Why I resist my past, yet dread my future.

His mother can't be known for that anymore. She can't be. She has to show him what real hard work is, what a real job is.

She has to show him what life he should choose. She has to set an example... She has to...

I break down for the fifth time this shift. I feel tears pushing at the corners of my eyes and I will them away. A customer hands me their card to pay and I can feel them accumulating, ready to dribble down my cheeks, ready to disgrace my face with humiliation, to show me up, to give away what is beneath.

But I never give away what is beneath.

I don't know which job is more degrading. One where I have to wear an apron at a checkout, or one where I have to wear...

Let's just say *Pretty Woman* made it look a lot more glamorous than it is.

A couple come to the checkout. The woman unloads all their shopping from the trolley. It's a weekly shop, and I can tell they have kids from the substantial amount of food. They buy the kinds of things I buy for my boy: fruit shoots, ice cream, tiny yoghurts.

He can't keep his eyes off me.

I know it's not because of my looks. I'm the oldest thirty-three-year-old there is. Sure, I'm not ugly I guess, but the baby weight clings to me like a joey in its mother kangaroo's pouch. Bags sit under my eyes like an eternal shadow. My hands shake under too much weight, tired from a life of abusing my privilege.

I've never been a drug addict. I was high-class. A thousand pounds an hour. But a high-class client doesn't make for any more pleasant desires.

But he's still staring at me.

And then I realise why. His face becomes familiar. And I sit here with the knowledge that could wreck his life and his marriage with one sentence from me.

He's still trying to figure out where from. He can't stop

wondering. I can see his thoughts trickling through his mind as he's trying to remember me.

Eventually, he speaks.

"Do I know you from somewhere?" he asks.

Yes. You do. You fucked me over your self-assembled Ikea kitchen table that you chose with your wife, after paying me in cash that she and your kid know nothing about.

"No, I don't think so," I tell him.

I continue scanning through their stuff.

He's persistent. If he realised where he knows me, he wouldn't be, but he keeps going. I almost want to show him. I almost want him to realise so she can know what a filthy prick he is.

"No, I do, I honestly do. I just can't place you."

"Maybe she's an ex-girlfriend," his wife jokes, and they both laugh that horrible fake laugh married couples do when they want to project an image of their perfect life onto others.

"No, wait a minute, I know where," he says, flashes of memory pushing to the surface of his thoughts. He probably has images now. Flickers of images.

Then it hits him.

And his mouth is suddenly open.

He doesn't know what to say. He doesn't want to tell his wife, but he doesn't want to let this moment pass. How brilliant. A woman he paid an exceedingly generous amount of money to shag now scans his chicken through the checkout, looking like a worn-down, crumpled piece of shit.

"You figured it out now?" I ask, part of me wanting to drop it, part of me wanting to show him up.

Part of me just wanting to get through this shift, but a bigger part of me wanting her to know what a scumbag he is.

"Er... No..."

"Yes, you have. I can tell. Why don't you say where it is you recognise me from?"

"Er," he glances at his wife, who slows down her packing of the shopping, intrigued. Then he comes up with a lie, and gives me wide eyes as a prompt to go along with it. "Your kid goes to my kid's school, right? Yeah?"

He widens his eyes at me, indicating to me I should take part in the lie.

"No," I say. "That's not it."

Part of me enjoys this more than I should. Part of me feels disgraced. This man has seen me naked. He knows what it feels like to be inside of me. He's fucked me hard. He's grabbed my hair and bent me over and tried slipping it into my arsehole despite my protestations. I hate him. I hate myself. I hate all of this. I hate this stupid job, my stupid life, his pathetic fucking lie and his pathetic fucking wife.

"You fucked me," I tell him, more venom than I intended. "And you paid a lot of money for it."

His wife pauses. She looks at her husband, perplexed. Lingers her stare upon his face, waiting for his reaction to either confirm or deny.

He bursts out laughing. A laugh that reeks of shame. An attempt to deceive his wife, to pretend that it's a lie, to convince her that I'm joking.

She turns to me with a face of disgust.

"How could you be so rude?" she asks.

Me be so rude?

Do you know what your husband did to me?

"I'd like to see your manager," she says.

And that is the end of that job.

❦ 18 ❦

MAYA

I'm in my room, kicking and screaming, making sure those cunts downstairs can hear me. Every step I take is a stomp, every object I lift is hurled, every breath I take is a loud growl that makes loose paper bustle.

My presence will be known. My anger will be acknowledged. This is SO unfair.

No one else my age has to do this. Everyone else I know can just go out in the evening without having to enter in a ridiculous confrontation with their pathetic parents. No one else is shut in their room like a slave, trapped in their confines, with no hope of escaping.

DICKS.

I hate them.

I FUCKING hate them.

I FUCKING hate them and I wish they would go FUCK themselves.

I'm sixteen, for God's sake. I'm old enough to legally have sex. I'm old enough to get married – with my parents' permission, which I'd never get, because they are total rejects.

Even though they can undoubtedly hear my anger, they can

definitely feel the roof above them shaking under my heavy steps – they still do not match my fury. Mum calls upstairs in her sweet singsong call, beckoning me:

"Darling, come say hello to your auntie Everly."

This only makes my wrath increase.

Partly because I am making my anger known, yet she calls upstairs like nothing is happening. Like she can't hear me.

And partly because she wants me to say hello to my auntie Everly.

Auntie FUCKING Everly.

Oh God I hate this woman, even more than Mum and Dad combined, times fifty thousand, plus infinity. She's pathetic. A mess. A disgrace against feminism.

I stomp downstairs. I'll see her, but I'm not going to be happy about it. I'll stand with my arms folded and my face in a scowl and I will look between them with eyes of hatred so they both know that they are lousy parents and are of equal standing as dirt.

"You see, I couldn't help it, and they sacked me," Everly is saying. She hears me enter, and she turns to me and smiles a forced smile. "Hi," she says. I can see her mascara running down her cheeks. For a woman in her early thirties, she sure does look aged. Her skin looks like someone who's had spots her whole life; there are so many acne scars I could practically do a dot-to-dot on their faded splodges.

She turns back to my parents and continues her melancholy diatribe about whatever fuck-up she's done this week.

"See, now I don't even have enough to pay the child minder when I get home."

Oh, and she has a kid. What a joke that is. No one even knows who his father is. He's a total social pariah. He has no friends, no life, and he plays with Barbies even though he's a seven-year-old boy. And everyone knows he's probably an AIDS baby.

I've met her, like, twice. She's never lingered her eyes on me for more than a few seconds. Honestly, if we woke up in a locked room together, I highly doubt she'd even know who I was. She'd just carry on being her ridiculous self.

"And I'm just so broke, and I'm so sorry to do this to you."

God, this woman is a state. I bet her body isn't even that unsexy, she just wears baggy clothes that hang off her like dead skin. A bin bag would be more stylish than that. And less greasy. And less ogreish.

URGH, I hate her.

"But, please, I don't know what to do."

You don't know what to do?

I know, kill yourself.

We all know she's a skank.

Everyone knows she used to suck dick for a living, but no one ever says anything about it. Make believe it never happened. Like she didn't earn money for taking it up the arse from rich pricks.

And we're all supposed to pretend like we're supportive. Like we're going to hold her syphilis-ridden hands and dance around the mulberry bush singing hymns.

No, we're not.

Because she's a train wreck.

Honestly, I can smell her body odour from here, and it makes me want to gag.

I bet she's homicidal.

No, really.

I bet if there was one person who was going to lash out, snap, and take everyone down with her, I bet it's her. I reckon she has a gun hidden away, just in case. She'll do herself and her son first. Then my parents, fingers crossed. Then all her clients – after she's fingered their arseholes for cash.

Honestly, she's such a mess.

I'm just waiting for it to happen.

❧ 19 ❧

EVERLY

By the time I get home he's already asleep. Drifting away to a world where money troubles don't exist. Lost in a sea of magic, away from realities adults have to face.

But I have to see him. I have to see his face. I need it.

After today, I really need it. To see what I'm doing this for. To see why I'm still bothering.

That sweet, young face. The face that reminds me what's important. What's keeping me from ending it. The only thing that stops me from taking the morbid escape.

His eyes flicker as I enter his bedroom.

"Mum?" he says quietly as I kneel by the side of the bed.

"Yes," I tell him, my voice soothing. "It's me."

I stroke his hair back and leave my hand on his head, trying not to shake, trying not to drip humiliating tears on his unblemished face. I smile dotingly at him. The beautiful product of my ill-advised life. The best mistake I ever made.

How am I going to support him without a job?

I already miss most of my meals so he can eat. So I can pay the rent. As long as he's fed, he's clothed, I can be content.

But now I don't even know how I'm going to manage that.

I can't go back to that life.

I can't.

Should I go back to that life?

Stop it.

It would be far more luxurious than this life now with that money. I'd earn in a night what I'd earn in a month.

Then again, maybe I'm missing the point.

I don't think someone would pay a thousand for me now. Not with my skin fading, my scars peeling, my cellulite clinging to my arse cheeks like a man with no boundaries.

I don't think anyone would pay anything for me now.

I'm worthless.

More so than they used to make me feel.

Back then, they just used to make me feel like shit.

Now I *am* shit.

"How was your evening?" I ask, my voice a hushed whisper. I don't want to wake him, but I don't want to leave him. I want to know everything about his day, his evening, what he did, what he said – I want to know.

I *need* to know.

"Good," he says, still blurred by his sleepy state. "Me and Janey played Mouse Trap."

I used to love that game as a child. I found it in Mum's attic when I cleared out her house after she died. The memories it brought back took me to a place far nicer than this one.

Now he plays it with his babysitter. Because I'm too busy working to be here. So I pay some teenager to play with my child.

Don't cry.

Please, don't cry.

I swore to myself I would never cry in front of him.

His mother needs to be strong.

But she's not.

But he still needs to think I am. I can't shatter the illusion. I can't let the mask fall. Because then I'll let the only person who looks at me like I'm their hero, like I'm worthy of their affection, lose all resemblance of faith in me.

I need him to love me.

"That's lovely," I say. "I just wanted to see you, go back to sleep."

"Okay," he says, turning onto his side and closing his eyes.

I nestle a gentle kiss upon his forehead.

"I love you, Mum," he whispers.

My body melts.

Why did he have to say that?

"I love you too, honey," I tell him. I mean it. God, I mean it.

I leave the room, though I hover in the doorway longer than he knows. He's asleep again and he looks adorable. My touchable dream. My greatest love. My greatest achievement.

My only achievement.

My favourite fuck-up.

I walk back downstairs.

Spend an hour staring at my computer screen. The monitor flickers, the way these old, thick monitors do. The tower hums loudly next to it. I tried selling this computer, but no one would take it. It's worthless.

People are scum.

They treat everyone like shit. Take the easy route to helping themselves. Rot from the inside until their rot takes the surface and they become the arseholes that they are.

In the end, we fight it, but we all become what we are.

Me, you know what I am. What kind of person I've turned out to be. There's no avoiding it.

But how far will I let my solace take me?

I could kill people. I could put them all in a room, trap them together, then sit in that room and force them to watch each other die. Because they deserve it. Because they should see the follies of their ways. Because everyone deserves it, everyone is worthless, everyone is a lying piece of scum.

But it's a far-off thought.

I don't have the guts to see such an idea through.

So I stare at the computer. Browse my way to the last site I wanted to click on.

I look on it.

I look at *Adult Friend Finder*.

And I offer my services.

For him.

Always for him.

❧ 20 ❧

2 HOURS, 23 MINUTES

Ashley, Everly, and Tariq all share the same look of shame. They shift their eyes nervously away from each other's glances, each considering what they have to say, and what they had to hide.

Ashley rereads the letter.

The same words are printed as the words he's read multiple times before. The clue is to figure out who has less to hide.

This is such a mind fuck.

He wonders, not for the first time, if it even is one of them who is the killer. If one of them actually did abduct them and put them there. Or whether these clues were just to toy with them, and if they were all going to inevitably die anyway.

Ashley glances at the metallic necklace and attached gun around Everly's throat. The gun fixed rigidly in place. The cannon pointed at the base of Everly's chin.

Then he thinks – it is strange. That something so large and noticeable was placed on her, and the rest of them just had blinking red dots.

It was overkill.

Maybe it was too much. Maybe she was trying to deflect

attention away from her by making her seem the most susceptible.

His suspicions grow.

"Right, I'll go first," Ashley declares. "I take steroids."

Tariq and Everly look oddly toward him.

"Well, we're going to have to see who has less to hide, ain't we?"

Hesitantly, the other two exchange affirmative glances. They don't so much nod, as share a look of sorrowful reluctance.

"I took them to get better at boxing, and I won my silver medal in the Olympics while on them. All of it, all those awards, all the cred I got – it's a lie. It ain't good, I know it, but that's what I got to hide."

He crumples up the note and throws it to the floor.

"Though I'm sure you could tell," he said, remembering removing his clothes and revealing the unfortunate side effects of the drugs.

"Time to come clean," he says, indicating the other two take their turn. "Who wants to go first?"

Everly huffs. Folds her arms, looks around.

"I got a kid," she says.

Ashley looks peculiarly back at her.

"That ain't something you hide," he says. "There ain't nothing weird about having a kid."

"If you'd let me finish," she says with a leering scowl.

Ashley raises his arms for her to go on.

"I got a kid, so I stopped doing what I used to do. I know I'm not much to look at now, but I used to be quite the catch."

Ashley wonders what she means. She may look a bit weathered, and is clearly a stress-head, but she is a pretty woman, and he finds it hard to understand how she doesn't see that. Still, it's not relevant, so he keeps quiet.

"I was an escort. And I don't mean your little scummy girl with fishnets hanging around on the street corner," she says defensively, and with a voice of spite, as if trying to read the thoughts of the other two. "People paid thousands for me. Sometimes, just for my company. Though most times, for more. Far more. It was..."

Her eyes glaze over and she stares at an empty space on the floor. She thinks about what to say next, then decides against all the thoughts that come to her mind. Explaining her career choice isn't what she intends to do to these two people. She doesn't need to give reasons for anything.

"I gave it up when I had my boy. That is, until..."

Her mind drifts, her eyes beseeching something in the distance that isn't there, a vague longing creating a weak haze in her faltering stare.

"Fair," Ashley says. "I get that. That leaves you, Tariq. What are you hiding?"

Tariq is already turned away from them, his arms wrapped around his chest, shaking his head. His eyes scrunch. His lip shakes.

"Tariq, mate, it's your turn."

"Leave me alone," Tariq protests.

"Why? Haven't you got anything to hide?"

"It's none of your business."

"Actually, not being funny or nothin', but in this scenario, it kinda is."

Tariq keeps his body faced away, but turns his head slightly toward them. He doesn't look at them, but his visage is just clear enough to be made out in the low light that casts shadows upon the contours of his expression.

"I am an honest man," Tariq claims. "I came here to do honest work, and that is what I have done. But some things are not–"

He stops himself.

He looks at Milo's body. His eyes had grown immune to the bloody stump at the top of the ageing man's chest. As if the exploded neck was a normal, average, everyday sight. And this acquired immunity scares Tariq more than anything so far.

He had never wished for something like this to happen to Milo.

Then again, that is a lie.

He'd more than wished it.

"Tariq, you need to tell us."

"I don't need to tell you anything."

His eyes remain on Milo. He knows he's going to have to admit it. Or blame will turn on him. And someone else will die.

"Then we know it's you, mate. End of."

Tariq shakes his head.

"You remember what the note said," Ashley persists. "Find out who is hiding something. We are all hiding something, but you seem to be the only one who won't spill. And we ain't got time for it."

"I am clean," he asserts without conviction. False malice overtakes his weary tears, and he wishes the ground would swallow him up and he could leave this situation.

Ashley and Everly exchange a glance.

"Tariq–" Everly goes to say.

"Fine!" Tariq grumbles.

Tariq turns his body toward them, but keeps his arms wrapped around his chest and his face pointed away.

"But you have to understand, I never threw the first punch. It was not up to me. *He* started it."

"That's fine, Tariq," Ashley assures him. "But we need to know."

Tariq closes his eyes and speaks.

❦ 21 ❦

TARIQ

S
trange, really. I feel so uncomfortable at this situation.
Not just because I'm scared – though I am terrified –
but because it highlights how much I can't seem to be
placed in any particular category of British person.

I entered this country decades ago, poor, and without
anything in my pocket. I built from there. Yet, even then, I did
not belong; I was an immigrant in a country in a recession with
an increasing amount of racial tension. I had no money, yet I
didn't even fit in with the rest of the poor; my skin made me
noticeably unlike them.

Now I am unmistakeably middle class. I own a pharmacy,
have a warm, generously proportioned home, and send my two
children to private school. Yet I do not fit in with the British
middle class, either. And I find that my children are ridiculed
for being the only children of Indian heritage in an elitist
school that charges me a sum of thirty-five thousand pounds
a year.

I didn't fit in with the poor, now I don't fit in with the
wealthy.

And do I fit in with other immigrants?

No. Because I no longer have the lack of wealth they come here with. My accent is no longer like theirs. I have been here for decades, and they look at me as someone who has everything and knows nothing of their plight.

I am always a minority.

So now I sit, in the backroom of my pharmacy, long after the closed sign has been turned, the shutters been drawn, and the sun sunk beneath the earth. With three young black men. And even now, sitting with other ethnic minorities, I feel uncomfortable and out of place.

It seems I do not belong anywhere.

I don't feel uncomfortable because of their ethnicity, I should add – what a hypocrite I'd be. It's because of everything else about them. Their hoods over their heads, their colloquialisms that I barely understand, let alone share, the glum look upon their faces, and the demeanour of intimidation that their slouched postures cast over me.

"I – I'm sorry," I stutter. "I don't really know what to say or do in this situation."

I am not lying.

I am not a strong, confident person. I've come a long way, achieved great things. I am proud. I am grateful. But I am in no way strong.

Someone threw a brick through the window of my business with a racially abusive note attached for the third time in a matter of months. The police told me they were too stretched to do anything about it, so I bent over and took their uncaring manner like they were lodging a giant pole up my backside, and I was thanking them for it.

My wife is in charge when I get home. The wife I met on my wedding day, mother of my children, that I have grown to love so much – she tells me when I need to mow the lawn, do the dishwasher, change the television channel. Hell, she even decides our bed time.

Do I long for it to be different?

Well. I am grateful for the life I have. I no longer face the poverty I grew up with, and I could never have dreamt of being in this prosperous position I am in.

As true as that is, you will notice that the above answer to said question did not contain a "no."

"Mate, there ain't nuttin' for you to do, like," the man sitting in the centre says beneath his black hoodie and purple cap, his voice not much more than a mumble. "You give us name, give us dough, we do him in, job sorted. You say nuttin' to no one and we ain't go no further beef with you."

It takes a few seconds for me to go through the man's words and decipher them.

"How much do you need?"

"Ten thou should do it."

"I will be right back."

I stand and walk my normal slouched stumble out of the backroom and to the counter of the pharmacy. I open the till and look at the money. More than enough. I have kept it there especially.

Then the ethical dilemma runs through my mind.

I know who it was. I saw the look on his face. I am sure of it.

But my money is not endless. I keep my wife, I send my children to school, but I do this by making sacrifices myself. Can I really afford ten thousand?

Then again, can I really afford not to?

The police aren't interested.

What am I supposed to do, hire security?

It would be cheaper.

But the image my business would create would be worse.

They will walk past my pharmacy and laugh. Two burly men stood outside the door to a drugstore. It would put off my customers, and that monster who keeps throwing the brick through my window will have won. He will see what lengths I have had to go to, and I can just see his face, cackling, laughing, chortling to himself as he saunters off.

No.

This has to be done.

I go back into the room and sit opposite the men. I hand the money to the man in the middle, who hands it to the man to his right. It's counted as the middle man continues to stare at me without changing his expression. It looks tough. Grumpy. Emotionless. As if he's cold beneath the surface. As if it's just ice, and nothing else left.

"Safe," says the counting man.

The man in the middle produces a pen and paper and hands them to me.

"Write the man's name down."

I do.

He takes it. Looks at it.

"Yeah, I know this guy," he acknowledges. "Been lookin' for an excuse."

"You know him?"

"What black guy don't?"

They stand up. Nod at me, which I only just see beneath his hood and cap concealment. They head toward the door.

"Be seeing you," I say in a pathetically delicate manner.

"No," the man says. "You won't."

❧ 22 ❧

MILO

The evening arrives and I have my tumbler of brandy,
filled a third of the way up. I feel its blissful sting
caress my throat and I relish its taste.

I sit in my chair. In the darkness. My television hasn't been
on for days, and that's how I like it. Too many people waste
their lives away in front of a screen nowadays, and I will not be
one of them. I have no interest in iPads, iPhones, and all this
iCrap. What's more, the news is full of slander against any
organisation I'm a part of, and I've had enough. Even the BBC,
who claims to be impartial and unbiased, labels us as 'racists.'
Even if it's not blatantly stated, it's inferred, and implied
through everything.

It makes me sick.

And I don't know what to think anymore.

One of them saved me. Saved my life. One of them, who
came from over there, from whatever land they come from, he
trained as a doctor through the British education system and
restarted my heart.

What am I supposed to think?

I still hate them.

Don't get me wrong, my ideologies aren't so weak as to be tainted by brushing against a positive experience with one of their kind.

But it poses an intriguing dilemma.

A thud against the front door shakes me out of my deep thoughts.

Just a single thud.

Clear, audible, unmistakeable.

But just one.

I rise from my chair, groaning as I do, feeling my bones already growing stiff from being sat in the one place for a prolonged period of time. I limp my way to the doorway, thinking this better be good, whoever is knocking on my door this time of the night.

It's too late for the postman. Even so, I didn't order anything. There's no reason for him to come.

I open the door.

A windy, blustery night with shots of rain firing diagonally against my driveway reveals itself. But no living thing looks me in the eye. The doorway is empty, as is the front of the house as I peer up and down it. An empty driveway, void of life, void of anything but weather.

Maybe there wasn't a bang.

It was probably just the wind.

I shut the front door and, almost in perfect synchronisation with its closing, a smash announces itself from the room I just left.

Now I know I heard that.

I go through the dark hallway as fast as my weakening body will allow me.

Bastards.

Someone threw a brick through my window.

The glass decorates my carpet with shards poking between the frays. The weather punches itself through the open gap. My carpet is already drenched, and my newspaper is already dancing on the gust.

But no one stands outside or inside it but me.

I pick up the brick. There's a note tied around it by an elastic band. I unravel it and display it at the perfect distance for me for my fading eyes to focus on.

RACIST SCUM

"FUCKING IDIOTS," I MUTTER. I HOBBLE TOWARD THE window, ignoring the discomfort of sharp glass that digs into my bare foot. "Come out, you sons of bitches! Come out and show me your face, if you got the balls!"

The front door opens and closes. Not a thud, not a knock, not even a doorbell – I clearly hear it open, then lock shut. The sound is indistinguishable from any other – the click of the handle lifting up to keep the door firmly closed finishes the sound, which is followed by a few footsteps through the hall.

Three hooded men adorned in balaclavas and tracksuits enter. One holds a cricket bat. One wears a knuckle duster. The other holds a knife.

I don't move.

I'm not scared.

I've faced worse than these amateurish dickbags.

"Give me your best shot, you pussies," I tell them.

I'm sixty-eight, going on seventy. I'm not about to back down for a bunch of home invaders who think they can beat on an old man for some kind of sick gratification, or retribution for something I never did to them. They can go to hell if they think I will show one smudge of weakness on my face.

That's the problem with this generation. They feel like they have some kind of entitlement. Like they are owed something by society.

I fought for this society.

I saw my friends die for this society.

My *fucking son died* for this society.

So they can grow up, tear it apart, and muddy it with their dirty hands. Ruin everything we built. Leave it to all the grubby foreigners to take it over, taking away everything that's ours, shitting all over our culture.

Kill me if you must.

I don't give a shit.

But you will not find me screaming or crying or shouting.

They walk forward slowly, surrounding me in a triangle. Standard intimidating techniques. They probably don't even know how to use those weapons they carry.

I see one of their hands.

Their black hands.

Holding the cricket bat.

Of course.

I laugh. Shake my head to myself.

If they found my dead body after this, it would only deepen my cause.

I lick my lips. Toughen my grin. Stiffen my posture.

Bring it on.

As if reading my thoughts, they all step forward and begin at once. The cricket bat wails into my kneecap, the knuckle dusters into my jaw, and the knife scrapes my back; enough that it will do nothing to permanently wound me, but will leave a lovely scar, like they were decorating a tree.

It isn't long until I'm unconscious.

I'm an old man. I can't take what I could when I was young.

I can still feel them beating me, even though I have no awareness. The pain is still there in my mind.

When I come around, the gang have gone. It's morning

again, and the killer has arrived to abduct me and put me in a room with four more arseholes.

I'm in and out of it, but they can't tell.

And I see their face.

For a fleeting moment, I see their face.

The one who does not belong. The one who put us all there. As clear as I saw those three arseholes surround me, I see them.

Then they shove a sedative down my throat.

And I saw their face when I woke up in the room with them.

I was in a room with them.

I knew who it was all along.

I knew exactly who it was.

I saw their face.

Then I died.

And I didn't tell them. I didn't tell any of them.

Why should I?

I knew who the arsehole was, but they owed nothing to me. My time had come enough times already, and I was anticipating my date with death.

But they will never guess who it is.

Never.

Because they are just too good.

23

TARIQ

Driving my son home from school. Driving on automatic, my leg bouncing anxiously. My head implodes. It rages and rants, from one stricken exclamative to another. I'm furious at the brick thrower. I'm livid at that racist fool. And I am disappointed with myself.

But I went through with it.

I was strong in my convictions.

What was I supposed to do? I say to myself.

I had no choice! I say to myself.

You're a fool, I say to myself.

I paid a good amount of money; this was not a spur of the moment thing. I thought it out – I can have no excuses.

I am to blame.

I just don't know if that's a good thing or not.

I realise my son has not been talking this entire time I've been ruminating. Just as distracted as I am. He's quiet in a strange way that I've never seen before. He stares at nothing. And I realise I've been so caught up in my own mess that I have failed to see my fatherly duties through – and when I realise that, it's possibly the most disappointing aspect of it all.

"Habib," I say. "You are very quiet."

He nods. Remains quiet.

He's never quiet.

Every day after school he's rambling on about this or that. He is telling me who he spoke to, what work he did, what his teacher said, how he reacted, what he thought – on an average day, he recounts almost every event that occurred at school in sufficient detail that I could almost act out the day myself.

Often my thoughts would go away then come back, and he'd still be going on, and I'd tune myself back into his recount of his activities and it would bring me such joy – such joy I didn't realise it brought me until a sombre silence replaced it.

His retelling of his day is the best part of mine, and I don't even realise he hasn't done it.

"What is it?" I ask.

Habib shrugs his shoulders.

"Hey, come on," I urge him. "I'm your father. You can tell me anything."

He sighs a sigh that raises his shoulders and pushes all the air out of his lungs.

"Hey, Habib," I say, my stern, serious voice taking over. "Come on. I want to hear it."

He takes a moment, holds his breath, then blurts it out: "Some boy at school was really mean to me."

Oh. Of course. I was wondering how long it was going to be until we had to have this conversation. It's inevitable, really, bullying – honestly, can you say you've never experienced it? Likelihood is that, if you had a room full of hundreds of adults and asked who was bullied at school, every hand would point to the ceiling. It's as common as breathing. Especially for a boy that will appear as different to the others as Habib.

I just thought he'd be a little older when it started.

That we would be afforded the luxury of time before we had to confront reality.

"And what did he do that was mean?"

"He pulled on my wrist and twisted it and gave me Chinese burns."

"Oh yeah?"

"Then he told me he should call it Paki burns because I'm a Paki."

That hurts. That really hurts. Like a dagger in my heart. It's a shame. Such a shame that we have to face such things when we are so young.

How does an infant school child even learn such a word?

An image of this bully's upbringing appears in my mind. Alcohol cans littered around their parents' feet. No one asking about their day. Never seeing their parents because their parents don't care. Too busy with drugs. Spending their money on tobacco instead of care for their child.

And I realise I'm stereotyping just as much as they are.

My son goes to a private school. These aren't drunken layabouts – but people who work hard enough to pay huge amounts of money for their child's education.

Yet, somehow, the child still learns such a word.

And I cannot understand how.

"Father, what is a Paki?"

I take a deep breath.

"It is a very offensive word for people with brown skin, and if it happens again, I want you to tell your teacher straight away, you understand?"

"Okay. But then he–"

He stops himself abruptly.

"Go on," I urge him. Although I don't want to hear the rest. I must, but I really, really don't want to.

"He kicked me. And it hurt."

I hate the kid who did this. I know he's likely to be very young, and a product of a neglectful home, but I hate him. And I want him to hurt. Hurt badly.

But I can't hire a gang for this.

That can't be my go-to for any time we face these difficulties.

Not for a child.

Not ever again.

Maybe my son just has to learn that this happens.

Maybe *I* have to learn that this happens.

The thought brings tears to my eyes, but I battle them away. I will not let them win. I won't.

"Can I ask you a question?" my sons asks.

"Of course."

"Is it okay for me to kick him back?"

I go to answer, then I don't.

What a question.

And tell me, honestly. What would you say?

Yes, kick that racist bastard back?

Or no, be the bigger man, and walk away? Then walk away again next time. And the next time. And the next time.

Until you end up like me.

A pathetic man with no confidence who lets everyone push him around.

Because he took the high road, and he walked away *every* time.

You know, if I'm honest with myself, I say I took the high road, but I didn't. I took the easy road. The high road is just a lie we convince ourselves of when we're too weak.

"I mean," Habib continues, "if someone says or does something really bad to you, it's okay to do something back, isn't it?"

As we reach traffic lights, I turn to him. His eyes, two sparkling circles reflecting the sun, stare at me with innocence this world cannot afford him.

He awaits my answer.

I know what I should tell him.

I know what I really feel.

I know what it's done to me.
And honestly, I do not know how to answer.

They taught me that love conquers all.

But in truth, love conquers nothing.

It's an excuse.

It's a word.

And a word is only as valuable as what the word hides.

❧ 24 ❧

TARIQ

I'm standing in the back amongst boxes of drugs, absentmindedly filling out prescriptions.

One of the girls from the counter brings me the next few prescriptions. I look through them and I see it.

His name.

He's back.

I stare at it for a little while. Pad the paper between my fingers, shuffling until it crinkles, feeling its crisp touch against my coarse fingers. In some kind of catatonic state, with no particular thoughts, just a hazy fixation on this name.

I peer out from the back. I see him waiting. Waiting all alone. A black eye. A cut across his arm. A bandage around his knee. He leans on a walking stick.

They did that.

No, I did that.

Did he go to the police?

No. He wouldn't have. Not him. His pride is too big. I don't know him personally, but I know him well.

I fill his prescription. I walk out front. I say his name.

"Milo Clunk."

He hobbles toward me and he takes the prescription, but there is a moment, a very brief moment, whilst I have one end of the packet of pills and he has the other, where we pause. Our eyes meet. There is a silence between us. It lasts for less than a second, but in my mind, it is stretched out into slow motion. Extended into a moment of... I don't know what. Just a moment. I see something behind his eyes, like he knows, like a score has settled, justice served, a silent understanding.

He was innocent.

He doesn't know that I'm guilty.

But in that look, deep in that look, there is a change.

In him, something has twisted. Maybe an ideology, or a belief. Something that makes the look on his face different in a way that is so subtle, yet so glaringly evident.

I can't put into words what it is, but I know it's something no one else has ever seen.

Then he takes the pills, turns, leaves. The bell above the door rings.

He exits my life.

❦ 25 ❦

2 HOURS 41 MINUTES

Tariq watches Milo's body as it slumps down the wall, gravity prying his limp torso from its precarious balance against the rusty surface.

Tariq's tears punch through his eyes.

"The police found the real culprit a few hours later," he admits. "It was a boy. Thirteen years old. Whose parents apologised and made him pay for it."

Ashley and Everly watch Tariq. Tariq remains focused on the headless body before him. He mourns the man he formerly thought had decided to punish him.

"He's a racist," Everly says. "It's easy to jump to conclusions."

"Yes, but that conclusion was based on nothing but anger, and now..."

"Now," Ashley confidently points out, "he is dead either way. And you didn't kill him."

Tariq doesn't turn his head.

"Maybe," he whispers.

"Let me ask you a question," Ashley says, thinking of something. "These guys you got to do him in. What'd they look like?"

"Why does it matter?"

"Just tell me."

Tariq sighs, closes his eyes momentarily to recall the image he'd rather forget.

"Three of them. All African-British."

"The one that sat in the middle – he wear a black hoodie? Purple cap?"

Tariq thinks for a moment, then turns to Ashley, both astonished and suspicious.

"Yes," he answers. "How did you know?"

Ashley shakes his head and snorts ironically. "That was my old crew, man."

"You were in a gang?" Everly says.

"Yeah, long time ago," Ashley replies, turning to Everly. "So there's a link between us, me and Tariq. What about you?"

"What about me?"

"How come we all link, and you don't?"

"What?" Everly protests, pointing an arm at Maya's body. "That's my fucking niece!"

"Yeah, but it don't make sense, does it? Surely the ones left at the end should all link. Why you got nothing to do with us?"

Everly's breath catches in her throat, her terror choking her.

"You're not suggesting–"

"I don't wish to be a burden," Tariq interrupts. "But the note did not say we were linked. It said someone was hiding something."

"Yeah, but we all know we're hiding something – steroids, employing gangs, being an escort or whatever. Maybe it's whoever has a link between us and is hiding it."

"Or," Tariq hypothesises, "maybe it means physically."

Tariq steps toward Ashley. Everly grows attentive, listening carefully, watching Tariq as he moves.

Tariq turns around and points out a red dot at the top of his spine.

"This is what will kill me," he says.

He points at Everly's unfortunate neck restraint.

"That's what will kill her. What about you?"

Ashley feels his body for something. Moves his hands up and down his chest, his legs, his neck, his head, just as he's already done multiple times. But they already know. He undressed in front of them, they know.

There is nothing on him.

"He's right," Everly concurs. "Why don't you have something on you?"

"Are you being real?" Ashley replies, his voice high and screeching, the anger from his long-gone days of gang warfare resurfacing.

"He's got a point," Everly says.

"If I was the killer, would I really make it that obvious? Surely this is a trap, or to mislead you or something."

"Maybe," Everly continues. "It's just that you've been the one to hand out most of the accusations so far. You made us undress, you made us tell our stories – why is it you have taken charge? What are you trying to achieve? What is it you're trying to manipulate us to do?"

"You kidding me?" Ashley turns to Tariq. "You buying this?"

Tariq hesitates, then moves his head into a gentle nod.

"It's the only explanation I have," he admits.

"Fuck you," Ashley says, raising his voice, jabbing a pointed finger in their directions. "Fuck the both of you."

"Right, that's decided then," Everly announces. "We believe Ashley to be the one who does not belong." She rotates herself, shouting at the ceiling and the walls. "We believe Ashley to be the one who doesn't belong!"

"Who you talking to if you think it's me?"

Everly says nothing. She and Tariq edge toward each other, creating a combined force, in case Ashley tries anything.

"You two are being serious, ain't you?"

They continue to watch him. Cautious. Wary.

Ashley glances at his watch.

"We don't got time for this. We got eight minutes, and it ain't me, I know that. We need to decide."

Tariq shakes his head, more and more vigorously.

"It's him!" Ashley says, turning to Everly and pointing at Tariq. "It has to be. Look at him, he's so prim and polite, he's got bottled-up rage. Look at what he did to the racist guy!"

"His name was Milo," Everly points out.

"It's him. Everly, please. Or we're going to die."

Everly looks from Tariq to Ashley.

His watch counts ever closer.

And the killer waits for the next death.

❦ 26 ❦

THE ONE WHO DOESN'T BELONG

I take Milo first.

    I take Maya second.

    I take Tariq third.

I watch him as he sits alone in his pharmacy, enjoying the blank space around him. It's night, and he's intentionally alone. He is away from his family, away from his children, away from any prying existence. He is as solitary as he can be – making it my perfect opportunity to begin my artistry.

Next, I need to decide in what order they will die.

I know that Milo will die second, after the incompetent, bawling child has gone. I'll definitely want her out the way, she pisses me off. But then Milo. I decided that the moment I met him. The rest will have little sympathy for him, and they will all target him with their accusations – meaning I need to remove him early on.

What's more, Milo deserves to die most.

Tariq – does he deserve to die?

I can see the puzzlement on his face. The conflict within. When no one is around, he cries.

So pathetic.

He wonders if he's done the right thing. Whether he's done what anyone would do. Whether he should be ashamed or pleased.

Little does he know that he's wondering the wrong questions.

After all, do you think he did the right thing?

Answer, in your head. Right now. Yes or no.

Did he do the right thing?

Got an answer?

Okay.

Your answer to that question is *not your own*.

Whether you have answered yes or no, you have done so because the environment you have surrounded yourself with has predisposed you to answer in such a way.

Think about it.

In England, only a few centuries ago, there were no televisions, barely anyone could read. The only entertainment you had was going to see the local hanging. Someone who was found guilty of stealing or adultery or something. Left out to snap by the neck. Seriously, read a history book – families would take picnics, it would be their day's outing, to go watch someone hang by the neck and suffocate until it breaks.

That is what you would do on a Saturday afternoon jolly. None of this cinema shit   you would go watch someone hang to get your jollies.

Whilst now you may go off to football or watch your kid play ballet or drink coffee with your friends or what have you – a few hundred years ago, you would have gone to the local courtyard. And you would have bloody *loved* it.

A few centuries before that, transport yourself to Rome, and you would watch gladiators in an arena fight to the death for the entertainment of those around you. Now you enter an arena to watch a sport where people fight over a ball. Tell me, is there really much difference?

The Bible teaches you it's okay to rape your wife. That it's okay to have a slave so long as you treat them well. That you should sacrifice your children for the love of your God.

Because at the time the Bible was written, that was okay.

So if you are religious, why don't you do that now?

Because society changed its mind.

Suddenly, it wasn't acceptable. But the words in the Bible didn't change – just the bits you pick and choose. Honestly, I don't understand why you bother having it in the first place.

The only reason you don't think it's okay for a man to rape his wife or sacrifice his kids to a vengeful God is because you live in a different time.

That is the *only* reason.

Say you are in a gang in London. Violence may be your way of life. You will believe that vengeance and retribution come from your fists or a weapon, and you will believe that Tariq did the right thing.

I imagine that you don't think he did the right thing.

Chances are, if you are reading this, it means you are someone who likes reading books. Statistically speaking, that would mean that you are a middle-class educated adult. That is the largest demographic of people who read books, so that is the statistically high probability. Therefore, you will not believe in such a thing as eliciting a gang to attack someone on your behalf as an act of revenge, as it is not 'proper' according to your upbringing. You teach your kids not to punch the bully back, but to walk away – which is preposterous, really, as this will only exacerbate the bully's attacks on your child.

I am not attacking you, or intentionally offending you – I am merely pointing out that you are only thinking that what Tariq did was right or wrong because of the right and wrong that has been forced into your mind from birth – whether it be from your parents, your teachers, your religion, or whoever taught you such a concept.

But such a concept of right or wrong is a manmade thing.

It doesn't exist.

You have made it up.

Your world has made it up.

Your politicians, religious leaders, cult maniacs, parents, role models, police officers, world leaders – they are the ones who taught you these values.

That there is right or wrong.

And you fell for it.

Like a sucker, you fell for it, you fucking moron.

There is no such thing.

When I kill a person, it is not *wrong*. It is not *right*. Those are labels *you* invent.

It just *is*.

That is all.

Two hundred years ago, make me a King's guard and send me to execute someone and what I would be doing would be seen as right. Someone tries to take my land, you wouldn't take them to court – you would fight to the death for it. And that would be seen as right.

So no, I do not think what Tariq did is wrong.

Or right.

But I admire him for finally having the balls to do it.

So I'll give him a fighting chance.

I'll let him die third.

2 HOURS 58 MINUTES

Tension rises in the captive's containment to a palpable state.

Palpable is an overused word nowadays. When describing a tense situation, it is always somehow 'palpable.' But, even so, there is no other way I can describe this box of aggression – it was palpable. And that palpability can make any room feel small. And when it's within a small, confined area, when death is the prize, and when the stakes are such that adrenaline has been racing through your veins for hours, causing a post-high weariness to surge your emotions to the boiling point – that is when tension gets to its most inextricably, definably, unequivocally palpable.

For Tariq, this was the first time he'd let his deep-rooted anger battle its way to the surface. Imagine you have a bucket with a lid that won't let any of the water out, and it's full within a month. Then it keeps getting fuller, growing and growing over the twenty years, but that water doesn't come out, it just builds, pressing against its containments – when that lid is finally released that water will flood your surroundings and spray anyone in the way of its wrath.

"Admit it!" Tariq shouts. "Just admit it! You've been doing this all along! You've been the one manipulating all of us! You've been the one—"

"You want to stop spitting on me?" Ashley retorts, wiping his face from the sprays of Tariq's projected saliva that came as a result of his uncontrollable words.

"I am not spitting!"

"Yeah, mate, you are. And I ain't being funny, but you're the one who's been all quiet, pretending to be a shy little bitch."

"I am not the bitch! You are the bitch!"

"Guys..." Everly says.

They both turn with unprecedented synchronisation toward Everly; this unprecedented synchronisation a contrast to the lack of synchronisation in their arguments. Everly raises a quivering hand and points it at the top of Tariq's spine.

"What?" Tariq says frantically, quickly dropping the argument, replacing it with sheer terror.

Ashley turns Tariq round.

The flashing red light fixed to his spine accompanies a beep. The ill-fated countdown they have come to recognise as a mortal omen has begun. In less than a minute, Tariq will cease to exist.

"What? What is it?" He knows what it is. He's just in denial.

Ashley ignores Tariq's cries and looks at his watch.

Thirty seconds.

It's not Tariq.

Those words fall heavily upon his thoughts.

It is not Tariq.

That means there is only one more option.

He looks at Everly.

Bitch.

An eerie silence bombards the room, allowing Tariq to hear the quiet sounds counting down to his death.

Tariq runs forward and grabs Ashley's collar.

"Get it off me!" he screams in Ashley's face. "Get it off me!"

"I don't know how!" Ashley helplessly replies.

"You put it there, take it off!"

"I didn't put it there!"

"Yes, you did! You did! Get it off me!"

Ashley sees the clock is nearly gone, and he does not want to be caught in the blast. With a sorrowful pain twisting his face, he pushes Tariq with the strength of a boxer to the far side of the room.

Tariq falls onto his back.

"You ba–"

His abusive retaliation falls short.

A rumbling explosion smacks through the back of his head. Tariq screams out, rolling desperately on the floor, revealing a broken spine sticking out of the base of his neck.

It didn't kill him.

The blast didn't kill him.

"Help me!" Tariq begs. "Help me!"

Everly and Ashley do nothing.

Just stand there as pointless voyeurs.

Not wanting to get caught up in anything else that could happen. Selfishly withdrawing themselves to save their own cowardly lives.

A second blast comes from within Tariq's skull, a hidden blast that fires through his brain and out of his eye. One of his eyeballs fires across the room like a basketball on perfect course for the net, bursting as it collides with the wall.

With a bloody face and a broken brain, Tariq's body falls with the weight of a rag doll against the floor, draping over the faded tattoos of Milo's legs.

At first, Ashley and Everly don't look at each other.

In turn, their eyeline switches from one body to another. Three dead bodies. Starting to stink. Starting to haunt their waking mind.

Even if they do get out of this, they will never be the same.

How does one recover from such atrocities? From witnessing such violent deaths? From being stuck in a room with them?

Their eyes raise from the death on the floor to each other.

Their steady, terrified eyes meet.

One of them *has* to be the killer.

And immediately, they both decide that they can't be mistaken in their assumption that the other is guilty of putting them there.

After all, they are the only two left.

You're as bad as I am.

You're as bad as I am.

You're as bad as I am.

You're as bad as I am.

You're as bad as I am.

You're as bad as I am.

You're as bad as I am.

You're as bad as I am.

❧ 28 ☙

THE ONE WHO DOESN'T BELONG

I diots.

If you haven't figured it out yet, you are dumber than they are.

It's obvious.

Isn't it?

Who I am?

And no, there's not going to be some great twist that I was another character that's appeared in the book – like I was one of the gang members who beat up Milo, or Milo's son back from the dead. How ridiculous that would be.

I have always been one of the five.

And now there's only two left, isn't it clear?

I suppose not.

I've had you fooled so far. I've had them fooled. And now the remaining is on its way to death.

I never lied. It wasn't a trick. I didn't play unfairly, so don't accuse me of that.

You probably think it's one of the dead, going to suddenly jump up and come back to life. In which case, get a grip, *they are dead.*

Dead dead dead.

Dead as a door nail, as Dickens once wrote.

Or do you still suspect some bigger twist?

Hell, I could be Everly's son. That could be it.

HAH!

What, a toddler?

Come off it.

Then again, this is a fictional world. I'm not real. I'm just a made-up character. These are just words written by the author, the prose of a character that some egocentric narcissist writer has created. I'm not even real. So, if you suspend your disbelief with enough imagination, you could see the toddler doing it, couldn't you?

No.

Maybe not.

But alas, you needn't. Because I am telling you now. I am not Everly's child.

I *am* in the room.

And it all comes down to this.

The final two.

How often have you changed your mind, out of interest? How often have you said, "Yes, I think it's that character," then watched that character die? Or suspected based on the information revealed to you that it may be another person within the story?

How often have you been certain? Maybe you are still certain. Maybe you do know, and are expecting a huge twist. Something radical. Something that will confound you for days.

Don't be an idiot.

It isn't complicated. Honestly, if you think about it in the most basic way possible, you'll know who I am. And you'll have seen what I've been doing all along. How I have set them all up. How I have made this wonderful world and wonderful game and been able to watch it all play out perfectly.

I thought I'd have to do more to manipulate the situation, but they tore each other apart with ease.

Now it's time to stop guessing, stop thinking you have it all figured out, and sit back and see who I could be.

And believe me.

It's going to be a cracker!

❧ 29 ❧

EVERLY

I've never really thought about power you wield in your hand when you hold a knife before.

You use it to cut carrots, spread butter, open a box. It's a utensil we all have in our home. It's something we use every day.

But we never give thought to the fatal consequences of just one false move of that knife.

You spread the butter, it slips, and it digs into your wrists.

You cut the carrots, you slam down hard, but you miss the carrot completely.

You open the box. Except you move the box and put your own child's neck in its place. Cut down. Then that child is dead. Night-night baby, hush-hush, sleep tight.

My child is asleep. Upstairs, asleep. Alone. Unaware of anything. Of what life has in store for him. The hard times he will have to face. The pig he'll likely become.

Because they all are at heart, aren't they?

I could end it all for him. Save him the pain and misery and sorrow life will inevitably deliver. Save him getting his heart broken. Save him getting sacked from a job. Save him money troubles.

Just one smooth flick across his throat and it would all be over.

Then I would be next. One swipe into my throat and I would gush blood all over the walls.

I wonder when they'd find us.

No one would miss me. But my son, maybe. Maybe when he doesn't come to school. Maybe the second day he doesn't go, when they can't get hold of me. Maybe the third day they send a police car round. They find us. Stale, crusted blood over two smelling corpses.

But why stop there?

Why just end it for us?

I could take more with me. I could kill the client I have lined up for me tonight. I could kill everybody outside in the street, walking past in their meaningless lives. I could run through the nearest town ending the misery of every racist, misogynist, fascist, villain and arsehole who doesn't deserve to be in this short, awful, non-existential existence that we wade through like steps through water and mud.

I could abduct them. Make them sit and watch whilst they die. Make them cry as their own guts fall out. Make them turn on each other. Make them witness their own downfall through the eyes of a stranger.

I could end it all. Prove who we really are. Prove that we are cowards who become bastards at the first sign of difficulty.

Don't tell me you're different.

You're all the same.

And I've had enough.

And that's when I stop. When I tell myself to stop these thoughts. When I remind myself that I love my boy more than anything in the world, and I would do anything to keep him safe.

I throw the knife to the floor and it takes a few seconds to stop clattering. I hold its handle like it's the tail of a dead rat and I place it in the bin. So it's away from me. So I won't do anything stupid.

And I get my makeup and my slutty, pathetic, demeaning outfit ready for the client. For my coming out of retirement. For the lesser amount of money I now charge.

And I will do what it takes.

And I will stop thinking about ending everyone's lives.

I will stop thinking about it.

I will stop.

I will.

I...

I could do it if I had the guts.

❦ 30 ❦

2 HOURS 2 MINUTES

"You," Ashley barks. "You! It's been you all along!"

Everly shakes her head, astonished pessimism taking over every piece of her: her face, her thoughts, even her cautious stance. She keeps her distance.

"Shut up," Everly says. "It's over. There's just two of us. There's no one else it could be but you."

"Get fucked, Everly. If that is your name?"

"That is my name!"

"Why'd you do it? Really, why kill all those people?"

"Stop it!"

"No, you stop it, you stupid bitch!"

A deadly impasse halts the dialogue between them. They try to figure each other out. Each of them certain that they are looking into the eyes of the killer, and each of them dumbfounded that the other is continuing their performance. That they are continuing to portray the part of a victim. That they still portray the image that they are not the one that put them there.

"Ashley, everyone else is dead. Come off it now."

"Quit it, for fuck's sake. Just let me go now, and I won't kill you."

"Kill me?"

"What do you want, me to wait another hour? It's done, you're left, it's over."

"Seriously, stop it. There's no point keeping this going."

"Fuck you!"

Ashley steps toward her. His fists clenched. His eyes watching her carefully. Waiting for a false move. Waiting for her to do something else, something deadly, something that will give herself away. Something that will give him the reason to kill her in self-defence.

"Stay away from me," she demands.

"Everly," Ashley says slowly and calmly. "I will kill you. Let me out."

"I can't."

"You can't?"

"Yes, because I didn't put you here, you freak!"

Another step causes Everly to back away, but she only finds the wall behind her.

"I'm stronger than you," Ashley points out. "Whatever you've done, however you've set this up, it's impressive, but don't forget – I am stronger than you. If it comes down to fists, I'll win."

"Seriously, please stop," Everly pleads. Tears sparkle in her eyes, then caress her cheek in a clingy drip that doesn't leave her face until it reaches the bottom of her chin.

"Turn off the tears."

"Leave me alone!" she wails, hysterical shrieking causing her voice to become frenzied and high-pitched.

Ashley takes another step forward.

"I'm giving you your final chance," he tells her.

Everly slides down the wall until she ends up on the floor, her arms around her legs, crying hopelessly into her elbows.

If she buries her head so she can't see him, can't see any of it, maybe Ashley will leave her alone. Maybe he'll let her go. Maybe he won't kill her.

"Final chance, Everly. Let me out or I am going to kill you."

Everly closes her eyes and thinks of her child.

Ashley gets ready to put his hands on her neck.

Why are you even reading this?

❦ 31 ❦

ASHLEY

A single lamplight casts shadows on the emptiest room in my flat. Darkness encompasses the corners most, reflecting my mind, my self-worth, and my soul.

I have never believed in souls. I had a brief fling with God when I was younger, but that was more to fit in with the guys I was with for approval – not priests or anything, but gangs. The tattoos and the big crosses and the prayers. I felt I needed to be a God-lover in order to do that.

Again, it's not that I don't believe in God.

It's just that I don't like him.

But if I did have a soul, and if there was a God who had that soul in the palm of his hands, those hands would be wretched claws. They would be coarse and rough, with cracked skin flaking over whatever sinful material they harvest. The finger-nails would be cracked – with broken nail over broken nail, produced from infection after infection, bruising that antibiotics won't solve.

And then that soul would be like the dark corners of my cell. A home for rats you cannot see. A ball of fire extinguished into ash by nothing profusely obvious, just flickers of water that turn out to be stronger than anything that burned before it.

Fuck you, God.

I know I sound dramatic. But you got to hear me out.

The only thing I ever did that Ma was proud of was winning those medals. She displays them with such glee. Sometimes she offers them back to me, for me to keep on my wall. But I don't want them. Because they are fake.

I injected myself for them.

I won them with cheap help.

Who knows if I'd have won them without.

Do you, God? Do you know? You, with your heightened sense of morality that allows children to die and murderers to live.

I'm being dramatic again.

This is my fault. I'm blaming some false deity, but it was my choice to do it. They were introduced to me, I was encouraged, and I was undoubtedly given a stronger nudge than my integrity could fend off – but I chose to take that needle. I chose to place it inside me. I chose to push down on it.

But what's worse, the complete disgusting thought I have to keep fending away from the front of my mind, the thought that projects itself like a cinema screen that burns the back of my eyes, that I am locked inside, and I cannot escape – is that I did it again. And again. And again.

Is that I still keep doing it.

I don't deserve any of this.

I'm a fraud.

I hear a clatter. Something falling in the hallway. My flat is small, and there's not much room for anyone to creep through. I'm sure it's something balanced precariously.

Even if it wasn't... Even if it was some arsehole come to kill me...

So what?

Fuck's sake, I am being dramatic. I should substitute the gym for a theatre group. Get over yourself, Ash, get over yourself. You're a grown man. No one ever owed you anything.

And you don't owe anyone anything.

Except, I do.

I owe those people that believed in me.

That cheered for me.

That painted the back pages with my face and declared me a proud representative of Britain.

I find a beer and I drink it. Then I drink the next one, and the next one, and the next one. I've pumped enough shit through my body not to care what it does anymore.

And when the beer is out, I find the whiskey. I'm a cliché. I'm the antihero in a noir film. A boxer who throws the fight, then goes and drinks whiskey. All I need now is some gorgeous femme fatale to come into my life and wreck it.

Within hours, I feel sick. I haven't moved from this crusty divot in this armchair and I need to piss so I just let it go. Why not? I live alone. The stink will be mine to put up with. Besides, I'm drunk. Isn't this what drunk people do?

Those shadows are blurry now.

They start bouncing.

I hear something fall in the hallway again.

But it doesn't register. I'm far too fucked for that.

I'm still, but the room is rushing in a circle that repeats on itself. I feel a burning need to vomit but nothing surfaces. There is three of everything.

God, I'm pathetic.

Blurs fight with the shadows and they move in a way I'm not used to. I hear something. Breathing, but louder. Footsteps, but muffled.

A broken visage stands over me.

"Is that you, God?" I joke.

I know nothing is there.

I know I'm full of it.

Still, it stands over me. A broken black image. Something disguised.

It tells me I'm pathetic.

Then another needle sinks into me. Into my neck.

Except this one isn't from me.

It's from the blur that fought the shadows.

❧ 32 ❧

THE ONE WHO DOESN'T BELONG

I stand over Ashley without even needing to disguise myself.

"You're pathetic," I tell him.

He just mumbles something about me being God.

He's right. I am like God.

I lean down and poke the sedative into his neck. He's so wasted he'll probably think it's another steroid. He falls unconscious faster than they normally do, but then again, he's wasted. He's almost passed out anyway.

Look at him.

Sat there.

All on his own. Moping about his own misery. I'd be understanding if this misery was forced upon him, but he chose it. He took his hand, wrapped it around the needle, and plunged himself into this spiralling mess that led to this pathetic wreck beneath me.

An Olympic athlete. Pah! He isn't a hero. He's barely a has-been. I wouldn't even label him a never-was.

He's a child who refuses to learn the lesson he's been teaching himself for years.

I pick him up, using all my strength, and he throws up over my shoulder. It's disgusting. I take my jacket off and throw it on the trolley.

An odour even more potent than the sick comes from him.

I see his tracksuit bottoms.

Fuck.

He's pissed himself.

It makes me regret choosing him, yet, at the same time, demonstrates that this sack of shit is exactly the right person for this. That he needs the lessons he's going to learn.

I get behind his head so he doesn't vomit on me again and I push him. It takes a bit of muscle, but I manage, and his body slumps onto the floor, half on the trolley, half on the stained carpet.

This place really is a shit-sty. I mean, I've invaded a fair few homes in my time, some of them exquisite, some of them divine, and some of them rat-infested sewer knapsacks – and this is as close to the latter as can be. So small it could be mistaken for a giant cupboard, decorations of the cheapest variety, and a smell like an old lady died, then came back to life and ate every rat there was before bringing them back up, then choking on them and dying again.

I pull his hefty body onto the trolley. His top slips up as I do this and I can see why he's so heavy. He is ripped. A good-looking chap, too – you know, without the sick on his mouth and the piss in his pants.

I'm not even going to change his clothes. He can wake up in that. Have everyone pity him as they size him up.

I wheel the trolley to the front door and into the back of the van. My driver thinks I'm moving to a new house. That he's helping me transport furniture. All I had to do was flash a cheeky smile, flaunt my tits, and they were putty in my hand. The things your sexuality can do, eh?

I kill him when we reach the destination.

I can't let him see where we are.

Hell, I'm telling you this story, and I'm not even going to let you know where we are.

It takes me a while, but I have everyone in place. I have to drag everyone by their feet, but that sedative would have put down a large rhino. I space them out evenly, shut the door, lock it, hide the key, and get myself in place.

Five chains around five ankles.

Three male, two female.

I put my game face on.

They are going to wake up soon and meet me.

And I am going to be the final one alive.

Have you figured out who I am yet?

Isn't it obvious?

Oh, it's too good.

It's just too good.

❦ 33 ❦

TIME IRRELEVANT

"**Y**ou bitch," Ashley throws at Everly, his voice full of venom.

He's figured it out now.

He's finally figured it out.

Everly is the one who does not belong.

He dives on her. Takes her to the ground.

She's going to have to die.

She put him there. She did it. She set it all up.

The filthy whore. The filthy, disgusting, vile little bitch. *The filthy excuse for a human being.*

She killed all these people – for this?

Filthy!

Everly struggles under his weight. He mounts her, placing his muscular arms over her, grabbing her wrists so tightly that her skin burns. His weight holds her down.

She thrashes and fights and kicks and throws her head and body around. She does everything she can do to get him off, to make it difficult for him to hold her in position, to do any kind of terminal damage.

She even screams, though she sees the irony of it.

If a scream would work, then it would have worked hours ago. No one is coming. No one is going to save her. She has to save herself.

"Get off me!" she screams. "Get off me, you fucking psycho!"

"You're the psycho! You're the one who did it all!"

With the two of them left, and Ashley's immediate attack on her, Everly could only leap to a similar assumption that Ashley had about her.

He did it.

Ashley lets go of her wrists and throws his hands upon her throat. He clamps them around her, squeezing tight. He feels his thumbs press down on her oesophagus. He presses harder. And harder. And harder.

She chokes. Wheezes an attempt to breathe, but he is restricting her oesophagus, holding firmly with his strong hands, denying her the oxygen she so desperately needs.

Those five fatal words present themselves to her thoughts with a striking immediacy:

I am going to die.

And it is true.

If she cannot escape from this, she cannot breathe. She will pass out soon. Then he will keep strangling and she will die.

She does everything she can with her body. Throws her hips up and down, punches her legs into the air as if she is drowning and furiously thrashing for the surface. Her fists, balled up into tight clamps, fight down upon his arms with an urgency that does not escape Ashley's awareness.

He fights through it, though her strength is inexplicably high.

It's what happens when someone faces a life-threatening situation, isn't it? They get stronger. They do things they could never do. Something about the mixture of adrenaline and foreboding and desperation that fills the body of even the weakest woman, giving them everything they need to do to survive.

Mothers have lifted cars to save their children.

Tiny daughters have lifted heavy fathers from the chair to carry out CPR instructed to them by 999 operators.

People have held their breath for extraordinary amounts of time, allowing them to plunge to the depths of the fatal lake and save their life-escaping baby.

And those symptoms are more evident now than ever. In Everly's persistent fists, they fight with superhuman strength against Ashley's triceps, biceps, wrists, deltoids, brachioradialis – everything she has is put into fighting the two arms fastened to her throat.

It isn't enough.

Her energy leaves as she's deprived of what her body needs.

She feels a headrush shake around her brain. A fluttering, lightheaded indicator of imminent death.

But she still has some fight left. Fight that she puts into her arms in a final strike against Ashley's elbows. That strike does enough to capsize his arms and allow her a sudden rush that she uses to escape his clutches. He snarls as he raises his gaze, looking at his victim's body crawl to the opposite side of the room.

But that was not enough to deter him.

He runs forward, retracts his arm, and puts all he has into a boxer's punch. He does what wild sexual experimenters refer to as a 'donkey punch', throwing his arm through the back of her head and knocking her out.

Her body flattens like dough under a rolling pin, spreading out across the floor.

He turns her over.

In her groggy state, she groans.

Upon the metallic necklace fixed to her collar bone is a gun, pointed toward her face.

Ashley places his hand around the gun, fighting through an awkward twist of the wrist to get the right position over the trigger. He bends his arm downward so as not to break his wrist from the force of the gun.

Then he pulls it.

Blood ornaments the wall behind Everly's skull with an image you would likely find in a Rorschach Test.

With no life left to control her eyelids, they open to reveal empty pupils. Empty, yet still staring up at Ashley.

A hole from beneath her chin to the top of her head hits Ashley hard with the reality of what he has done. It's long enough and thin enough to fit a cylinder tube, should one be demented enough to wish to do such a thing to a corpse.

34

EVERLY

It feels strangely familiar, dressing like this again.

I try to hide the feelings of humiliation, regret, and hopelessness – instead, replacing them with feelings of nostalgia. Like I'm going back to a place I haven't been in a while.

Only, it's a dangerous situation. It always was.

And I have to remind myself what I'm doing, because I still can't believe I've given myself permission to do it.

I am going to have to have sex with a stranger for half the price I used to charge.

I mean, I'm not that old, am I? Thirty-three? Your thirties are meant to be your sexual peak for a woman – or so all those ridiculous magazines say. Then again, the last edition of a woman's monthly magazine I read debated whether it was stupid for a footballer's wife to use a coupon in a supermarket. Honestly, I'm not sure if their superficial declarations and debates are ones that I'm going to pay an entirely huge amount of attention to.

Still, it is a little shitty. That I'm not charging what I could when I was nineteen. Maybe if I took the MILF angle, and marketed myself as an older woman, then...

Stop it.

I'm talking as if this is a permanent venture. Like this isn't a singular event.

I have no choice.

Just this once. To keep me going until I find another job.

To keep a roof over the head of a precious little boy at home.

Though I tell myself, again and again – I could end this. For me. For my son. For any stranger who is not deserving.

For this client.

This client.

That I am about to fuck for money.

As the lift doors close before me, I bow my head and feel shame. What would my son say? If he were able to grasp the concept and treat it with the maturity of an educated adult, would he really condone what I'm doing? Would he want that for me?

I don't have a choice.

He needs to eat.

I can go without. I have done so numerous times. I've learnt not to need much to fill my appetite, but I couldn't do that to him.

In a sudden moment of panic, I press the buttons on the lift and my mind goes into a foggy blur.

I thought I'd be worrying about how degrading this is. About how pathetic I am, about how I'm going to have to bend over and take it from another heaving scumbag with too much money. About how disgusted I'll feel to have him inside of me, to have him fill me, pushing through my dry cunt, rubbing my insides like wood against metal.

But I'm not.

I'm thinking about how my son would judge me.

Would I even be able to give this client the experience I once could?

I'm not what I once was. I can't stimulate conversation in the way I once did, energise small talk, imply innuendos. I can't entice men in the way I once managed. I can't dress provocatively without revealing a stretch mark from pregnancy or a wrinkle from stress or some other deformity or degradation of my body or disgusting change that age and circumstance has done to me.

What about when they see me, if they don't want me?

If they ask for their money back?

If they take off my clothes and look at me with a face of disappointment?

That look of a child on Christmas morning when they are expecting an Xbox One, and get a pair of socks.

Is that what I am now? An unwanted pair of socks?

I tried dating a man once. About a year ago. Figured my son could do with a father figure. Lasted weeks. He took my clothes off and saw the scars from years of self-abuse and described me in the way that all women dread being described.

"You are damaged goods."

He dressed and left the house without looking at me.

I cried myself to sleep that night, but it wasn't any different from any other.

I cut myself on my thighs so my son will never see it.

What about those marks?

What if it's a man who likes legs?

I have to turn back.

I can't do this, I have to turn back.

And just as I think it the doors open, and a corridor of hotel rooms is displayed before me. My legs are unknowingly carrying me forward, pushing me through as if aimlessly forging against a rising tide.

My energy is gone.

I cannot do this.

And just as I make that decision, my hand is knocking on the door of room eighty-three.

"It's open," comes a voice that sounds surprisingly different to what I was expecting.

It isn't the voice you'd expect from your average client.

I open the door and it creaks into the room. It's a large, lavish room, decorated with grand ornaments and fine architecture. Even the windows take up most of the wall, parading down upon the stylishly floral bedsheets tucked perfectly into the sides of the bed.

"Hello?" I say.

"I'll be right out," comes the peculiar voice again. Like it's feigned deepness, someone putting on a low pitch. Someone pretending to be a middle-aged man, who is clearly not.

"Erm, where are you?"

"Money's on the dresser. Help yourself to a drink."

I look to the dresser, a large set of drawers with a mirror on top, next to an envelope and a tumbler of whiskey.

Just what I need.

I walk over to it and glance at my reflection. The light hits it in the perfect way to highlight the flaws of my skin. It's one of those mirrors positioned in a way that would make even the most beautiful of people feel inferior – which means it makes me feel like dirt.

I pick up the envelope. Open it. A wad of cash is inside. I'll count it later.

For now, I need to drink.

I pick up the tumbler of whiskey and gulp it down in one. Its sharp sting makes my throat know it's there, but it's–

I lose my thoughts.

I stumble.

I fall.

I'm on my knees.

The bathroom creaks open.

I'm on my knees.

I've fallen.

I stumbled.

I'm on my...

Feet appear, blurred, hazy.

I fall onto my front.

When my eyes next open, I see four other people with chains around their ankles, in a room where I am held captive.

This isn't real.

Stop lying.

35

TIME UP

Ashley looks at the corpse he created.

He thought he'd feel worse than this, but he doesn't.

He feels numb.

Empty.

Like it was something he was meant to do. Like he couldn't help it.

Like he had no choice.

Because she was the killer.

And just as the thought engrains itself permanently into his mind, a rustle comes from behind him.

And a foot is twitching.

My foot is twitching.

And my eyes are opening.

36

ASHLEY

I still feel a needle digging into my neck, even though it isn't there.

I'm being wheeled along on something.

Above me, lights pass.

I have no idea what's happening. My eyesight is a mess of colours entwining into various luminosities. Contrasts and hues change from their various extremes.

I am travelling.

I lift my head momentarily, but it's heavy. It feels like gravity has increased, like a set of weights has been rested on my forehead.

Has my coach done this?

A punishment, maybe?

My thoughts lack clarity.

What's happening?

I am dumped onto the floor of a room. Something cold and metal is clamped around my ankle. Someone is doing this. Someone must be doing this.

But who?

I try to open my eyes. Try to understand. But it's like driving through fog. Somehow, I'm moving forward, but I can see nothing. Somehow, lights punch against me, but I can barely see those lights in front of me. A heavy peace weighs down my body, and for a moment I believe that strings are tied around all my limbs and a puppeteer is controlling my movements.

I close my eyes again and go out of it.

When my eyes open in their next dozy haze I can tell there are others. I can't see them, but there are others.

And I never remember this until I kill Everly hours later. It doesn't become apparent to me until it is too late that I saw the killer's face.

I saw it.

Fresh, flickered with blood, freckles and pimples and everything you don't expect.

Clear.

Dragging me.

Blurred, but with features unmistakable.

My head lifts and they lock something around their ankle. A restraint.

I pull on mine.

I have one too.

Why do they have one?

And I look them in the eyes.

And I look *her* in the eyes.

She looks too young to be able to do this.

Surely it can't have been her.

"What..." I try to say. "What... are... you..."

She puts her finger in front of her mouth, looks me in the eyes, and shushes me.

If only I remembered this before I was the last one standing.

If only I remembered that I saw her face.

Her face.

The face of the one who does not belong.

The face of an evil, sick, and twisted sixteen-year-old girl.

❧ 37 ☙

TIME GONE

Ashley's memory hits him harder than any opponent ever has.

It doesn't register at first. It feels false. Like it's something he created himself. Like it's something someone placed into his unconscious, like a DVD into a DVD player, and allowed its fakery to play in his mind.

His head slowly turns over his shoulder.

She sits up.

"What the fuck..." he mutters, but it does nothing to him.

It doesn't give him any resolve that could allow him to move from his static position. His feet are rooted to the floor like roots of a tree had twisted themselves around his ankles with such force and tremendous vertical pull that his feet could not lift if he wanted to.

Nor could it do anything to remove his utter horror at the revelation that he has just killed an innocent woman. That, all along, the killer was in this room, but playing possum. Pretending to be dead with a performance that an ardent Oscar-winner would not fail to be proud of.

A little girl. A child. A sick, twisted teenager.

How could it be so?

She rubs her neck, twisting it from side to side.

"I tell you what," Maya says. "Lying in that position for so long has given me a real crick in the neck."

"You..."

Ashley attempts to launch himself into a tirade of abuse. The words form in his mind: that she is a bitch, a psycho, a sicko, a demented monster, an underage rabid animal. But none of those words form on his tongue. All that forms is a stutter replaced by a sickly quiver. His stomach lurches, his body fails, and his mind is awash with emotions that do nothing but cloud his judgement and make him fail to move or act.

She takes a key from her back pocket and undoes the restraint around her ankle.

She has a key.

A key.

All along.

She has a fucking key!

Ashley's ability to move comes back in a sudden bombardment of energy – if this were a movie, this is the point that a camera would launch itself downward toward his face to symbolise a sudden twist in gumption, a change in his demeanour from that of saddened horror victim to vengeful aggressor.

He runs forward.

Maya doesn't even move. Because she knows what points of the floor his ankle restraint can't reach. She knows how far Ashley's restraint will allow him to move. She planned this well.

And, as she stands against the far wall, his outstretched claw pushes a gentle breeze into a strand of hair that sits loosely over her face.

He swipes and reaches and pulls and yanks on his ankle restraint. Does everything he can to get to her. She sighs, watching him with a cruel, knowing smirk that only incenses him further. She even tries to steal a glance at his watch to let her know how long he has been at this helpless attempt at a failing attack.

After it becomes apparent that his hostility is restrained to a short radius of the room, he halts, breathing heavily. He can't think. Can't talk. Can't move or act. He is consumed with rage. Completely taken over by an animalistic need to kill her and maim her and put her through every piece of sorrowful suffering that he has endured.

He's killed a person.

An innocent person.

"I know, I know," she says, lifting her arms into the air in a playful shrug. "Genius, I am."

He screams like a feral beast. He can't even turn his abuse into words anymore, he is forced to growl, forced to act like a caveman who doesn't understand enough to communicate in English.

"If it helps," she says with a slanted smirk that continues to rile him. "She was going to die next anyway."

He roars again.

"If you could give that a rest, then I can answer any questions you may have."

She crouches. Her hands knock on a hollow part of the floor that had previously been below her body. She lifts a hidden lid, where a gun has been placed.

Ashley's eyes widen.

A gun had been hidden beneath her all along.

"I know what you're thinking," she says as she stands, releasing the ammunition, checking the bullets are still there, then placing them back inside the gun. "How could you be so stupid, right?"

He shakes his head. Tears fire down his cheeks like rapid bullets. She sees every emotion fire through his face, like she is flicking through the pages of a book that have a different expression drawn on each.

She cocks the gun.

"Then, after Everly dies, I was going to give you another hour to figure it out. But then, you probably still wouldn't have, would you?"

He closes his eyes. Bows his head. A mixture of sweaty shame and pent-up rage, neither of which he is able to channel or direct into anything of any use.

"But you didn't. You didn't even suspect. You didn't have a clue."

She sighs. Looks at him with raised eyebrows, as if she were a teacher and he just handed her a piece of work that was completely not what she was intending to receive.

She points the gun at him.

He screams again.

"Honestly, you're not a child or an animal, could you speak properly?"

"You fucking bitch!"

She rolls her eyes.

"Yes, then again maybe you shouldn't bother speaking. Your contribution really wasn't useful."

"How did you – why did you – what did you…"

"Do you want to pick one of those questions, or do you want me to answer them all?"

He shakes his head. Coherent thoughts fire through his manic brain like a word jumble he was beginning to figure out.

"*Why?*" he says, louder than he intends.

Maya shrugs her shoulders and grunts an intelligible, "I dunno," at him.

Ashley shakes his head.

"You mean you don't even have a reason?" he whimpers.

"Why did you take steroids?"

"What?"

"Why did you take steroids? Why did Milo join the EDL? Why did Tariq employ a gang to beat up an innocent veteran? Why did Everly decide to fuck her way out of poverty?"

"So this is teaching us a lesson?"

She laughs loud, and she laughs hard.

"I don't care about lessons. Hell, I go to college, I hate them."

"So why?"

"Answer my question first. Why did you take steroids?"

"Because – because I wanted to win."

Maya makes the sound of a buzzer signalling the incorrect answer on a quiz show.

"Nope, try again."

"I just told you."

"You stood in a gym full of boxers," Maya points out, "And you looked around, and what did you think? What did you say? How did you act?"

"They – they were bigger than me. My opponent was stronger. Quicker."

"And when you were on the Olympic team, I watched you on TV."

"I–" suddenly, the clue falls into place.

"What did you think at the time?"

"I thought – I thought, they are better than me. I thought... I do not belong here."

Maya stays silent.

"Why does that mean you need to kill me?"

"None of us belong, Ashley. But that doesn't mean we shoot our bodies up with shit."

"I don't understand why that means you need to kill me."

Maya shrugs, points the gun and shoots.

❧ 38 ❧
MAYA

DICKS.
I say it again.
My parents are DICKS.

I sit in my room and fume. Still angry that they won't let me go out with my friends. Still angry that they have confined me to their house.

They think I am just some innocent little girl. A timid sixteen-year-old who barely says anything in college. Every parents' evening it's the same – "I wish she would come out of her shell," "You should volunteer more in class," "You don't contribute much."

True, I say nothing. And it makes everyone worry about my crippling shyness. That I'm never going to come out of my apparent shell, like I am some bloody turtle.

You wouldn't want to see inside my shell.

I own this fucking shell.

Inside it are all the thoughts I hide. The desires you don't know about. The things my parents would dread if they found out the truth.

The other day a boy looked at me. Kind of cute, messy

brown hair, brown eyes, prefect skin, athletic physique. He looked at me and probably thought, hey, she's kinda quiet, but I dig it. I could ask her for her number. I could take her on a date.

He smiled at me. Like he wanted to get to know me.

I imagined myself digging a corkscrew into his muscular pec and opening up his nipple. I saw my hands grabbing hold of a Bunsen burner from the corner of the classroom and setting alight his rugged hair. I could depict perfectly the action in my mind of me going up to him, grabbing my young fist around his scrotum, laughing in his face so hard as the weak skin holding his testicles in place detaches and the coil wrapped around his bollocks unwraps until its dangling freely by his Converses that cost far more than his parents could likely afford.

And he was looking at me.

Like I was normal.

But I am normal.

It is he that's odd. He denies this. You all do. You deny you think this.

And I won't take this anymore.

I have a desktop on my desk in my bedroom. Yes, a desktop – who even has one of them anymore? Me. Because my parents won't get me a laptop. It still has Windows fucking Vista on it, it's pathetic.

So I rip the desktop out of the wall, bringing the socket off, but I don't care, I really do not care what damage I do to the precious house they all worked so hard for.

It will be mine soon, anyway.

Even that stupid bomb bunker below the house.

It was a ridiculous waste of money. Dad is so innately paranoid he built a fucking bunker in place of the basement, but he won't splash out to get me a computer that takes less than fifteen minutes to load.

I mean, a bunker in the basement. He has laden each wall

with metal. With *metal.* Why? Because he has some kind of mental disorder which means he's paranoid.

Paranoid?

Arsehole.

I carry it in both my hands. It's heavy, but it doesn't matter, I can take it. I drag it down the steps, one bump at a time, announcing my presence.

Mum appears at the bottom of the stairs, shrieking at me like a retarded banshee.

"What are you doing?" she says in a pitch so high she could be mistaken for a character David Walliams would write in one of his books were he in acid.

Without any hesitation I bring the computer tower up to head height and swipe downwards across her face like I was swiping left on tinder. She stumbles to the ground, goes to shriek some more, and I hold the tower up high and bring it down and fire it into her head so hard that this time she does not get up.

I mount her. Sit over her back. Take my position. Hold it up high and smack it down again.

And again.

And again.

And again,

And again.

And afuckingain.

Until her face is surrounded by a pool of blood that spreads across the carpet, sinking across to the wallpaper, until it spreads to the nearby door, staining the wood with my liquid trophy.

"What is going on?" I hear Dad's over-middle-class accent demand with the ferocity of a puppy and the fortitude of a fucking imbecilic mouse.

A fucking idiot mouse with a fucking idiot head and no

fucking legs because he's such a fucking moron I FUCKING HATE HIM.

But to say this is a crime of passion would be a lie.

I'd been planning this in my head for ages.

Dad will take more than the computer tower. I heave into the kitchen, taking a knife out of the cutlery drawer. I hear his childish shrieks as he discovers his pathetic wife lying dead on the floor.

I'm behind him digging my knife into his spine before he can even think to dial 999 and I watch his entire body paralyse just paralyse fall apart fall down until he is void of moving ability and his fucking cock will remain limp forever.

I stick it into his back again. And again. I count how many times I do it, but I stop at thirty, as I don't want to be a boring mundane cunting parasite like they both are.

He's limp but I have to make sure so I turn him over and blood comes out of his mouth pouring down his cheeks and it annoys me that it gets on my jeans because they are my jeans I bought them from Gucci and I fucking love Gucci because I'm not cheap like this dying-nearly-dead arsehole below me and I want to hurt him more just because I can just to feel the full validation so I stab him again but this time in the face digging it into his cheek and dragging it through his jaw until it grates his teeth and I can hear the steel following the top of his gums and I take the knife out and I go wipe it on his stinky wife because she should have to deal with his blood not me not me not me she should because she's the passive-aggressive boring housewife whore who married the filthy prick and they are so pathetic so I stick the knife into his throat and leave it there but it doesn't matter that I do because he was dead long ago. And I. Hate. Him.

I stop.

I breathe.

So angry. So riled up.

I think what to do next. Where to hide them. Where to put them.

I leave them for now.

No one will miss them.

There is a metallic bunker below me.

And I am bored.

And I have started the killing.

And I don't want it to end yet.

Hush.

It's over now.

✣ 39 ✣

THE ONE WHO DOES NOT
BELONG

A nd it is prepared.

They lay down before me like a bunch of helpless children. Funny, I am the youngest, yet they are all bowing down to me.

And what, you knew it was me all along?

Or did I throw you by being all like, "I take Maya second," back in the middle of the book? You thought because I spoke about capturing me, that I wasn't lying?

I said that someone standing up from being dead was a ridiculous idea. And I bet you fell for it. HAH! You're as much of a fool as my parents.

Aw, don't feel hard-done by.

This is a made-up story, I can do and say anything I want. It's my story, so I can decide to say whatever. Doesn't matter if I was lying. So stop your whining.

You're ruining my brilliance.

Though as brilliant as I am, I'm in a room with far bigger narcissists than I could ever be.

The note, left in the middle of the room.

The second note I hid within my underwear, to be released when they are so absorbed in their panic that they don't pay any attention to the genius corpse that grins inside.

Then I have to ensure that they will all die.

For me, a dud that I place over my heart.

For Milo, a small explosive at the base of his skull.

For Tariq, an explosive to his spine.

For Everly – well, hers takes a bit more effort, and it takes me a good fifteen minutes to do it. I get so worried they will wake up, but I've got them sedated pretty heavily, so there's no risk of that. Not until I want them to. So I take my time on her. Digging the claws of the necklace into her collar bone. Fixing the gun in place; so it's pointed at the base of her chin. It's a thing of beauty.

She is going to be terrified. And I'm going to get to watch.

My loser aunt. The skank who fucked her way through her twenties. At least her kid will get to go to a foster home, or get adopted, and grow up with someone better than this shit-stain for a mother.

To my left, Ashley. He gets nothing. Not yet, anyway. Not yet, as I hide a gun beneath the floor in an unmarked hole that I will lie over once I feign my death.

They are all disgusting people.

All people who deserve this.

And I look around at them and remind myself of it.

Ashley. An idiot boxer. A pathetic excuse for an athlete.

Milo. A racist. Simply because someone of a certain religion and ethnicity killed his son in a war – and I mean, not being funny, but what did they think was going to happen to him in a war? – and he got all hysterical about it. I mean, seriously, Jesus, I'm a fucking teenage murderer and already I know what's wrong with his logic. Perhaps I could look at him and think all prejudiced pricks are in their late sixties, and judge every new pensioner the way I judge him. What a moron.

Tariq. Ah, Tariq. He sits next to the racist. Perfectly positioned for a barrage of ridiculing. Milo is a clueless old bloke who doesn't remember much, so he won't remember where he knows Tariq, he won't remember who filled out his prescription to keep him alive – but Tariq will remember. Tariq will know why Milo belongs next to him. He'll know why he's there. Though, being the easily-intimidated bumbling mess of a man he is, he won't reveal it until he's truly pushed. By then I'll be dead – well, pretend dead – and I'll get to listen to him bare his soul. And I guarantee that point will come.

And Everly. Oh, Auntie Everly. She's my favourite. I almost had sex with her. And, when she turned up in my hotel room, honestly, I nearly did. What a beautiful woman – but only beautiful because she's beautifully flawed. I didn't pick her because she's an escort, or a struggling single mum. I pity her for her difficulties in life, and I don't really feel much beyond either contempt or sexual gratification toward anyone that I meet. I picked her because she belongs with high-class escorts, yet refuses to understand why.

Because flaws are wonderful. That little wrinkle above her nose, that little stretch mark on her stomach, even that curved scar from the broken glass of the photo frame she smashed and used to carve her pain into her skin – those flaws are what I would love her for, should I feel anything other than contempt for her. And she's ungrateful for them. And so she deserves to die.

And then there's me, the one who does not belong.

I take a few pills of Tetrodotoxin.

If you don't know it, look it up.

It's a drug that slows your heart right down to fake death. I take it now, knowing that when they attempt to revive me in little over an hour, they will believe that they have failed, and that the one who doesn't belong is dead.

Why don't I belong?

I've explained why these people didn't belong – honestly, if you haven't understood why, do try to keep up – but I haven't explained why I do not belong.

Let me ask you a question.

Have you agreed with anything I've said?

I've told you about how there's no such thing as right or wrong. That even killing is judged by the principles of the time and society we live in. That it's not right. Or wrong. It just is.

Do you agree with that?

I've told you right from the get-go that human nature fascinates me. I wanted to see what would happen when I put these egocentric sycophants in a confined space together.

Isn't that why you bought this book?

Because *you* wanted to see what happened too?

Honestly, why else would you have bought it?

You bought this book because you wanted to see what happened when five people were put in a room and left to die – just like I wanted to see when I set it all up.

See the similarity?

Or maybe that's not why you bought it. Maybe you aren't as desperately eager to understand the morbid consequences of a person's fatal actions.

Or then again, maybe you are?

And my other adamant, stubborn, hopeful message my supposedly narcissistic mind will give you – my mind that I am sure doctors will label deranged, simply because you can't be diagnosed with a personality disorder until you are in your twenties. Wonder if that is the same with psychopathy? Surely not. I am no psychopath.

I am a bastard.

And that's what my other message was. Remember?

That all people are bastards.

If you were placed in a room with four people and your life was about to end, wouldn't you be a bastard?

If you were Ashley, and Everly was the final person, would you not kill her for your own safety? For your own sake?

Not going to piss about here – apparently killing someone makes you a bastard. Your society dictates such a notion. That means that I am in turn a bastard.

Or a psychopath, whatever.

I am sure that none of these things make sense to you. In fact, I am positive of it. I would go out of my way to swear that you would not entertain such ideas, nor would you conceive of such concepts, or believe such farcical assertions.

But if you do.

Maybe, just in the slightest.

And you're prepared to admit it.

Then maybe you are just like me.

Judged. Forced to keep your controversial opinions to yourself. Never allowed to share your insights because they scare people. Never allowed to be so stubborn or straight-forward with your opinions.

Does that sound like you?

I hope not.

For your sake.

And hopefully you are about to put this book down, think it's nonsense, slate it to all your friends or, if you don't have any, slate it on social media (which inevitably those true egocentric narcissists in need of validation will do), think this book was a steaming pile of pointless shit, stand up, walk out the door, and ultimately carry on with your life. Ranting about how crap that book you just read was to a partner who doesn't really care. Because they don't. No one really cares. Not if you are as boring as everyone else in the world.

But, then again, you may not be, might you?

Because maybe, just maybe, you have been sick enough to find these notions perceivable...

Maybe you have enjoyed my sick little games...

Maybe you are just as fucked-up as I am...

Maybe, just maybe, after all of this – it is you who *does not belong*.

HAVE YOU ENJOYED THIS BOOK?

If so, why not join Rick Wood's Reader's Group at
www.rickwoodwriter.com/sign-up and get more of his books
for free?

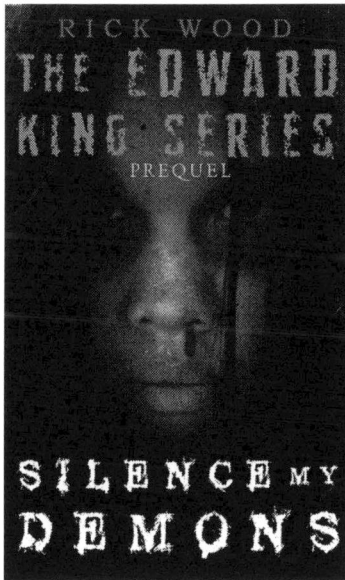

ALSO AVAILABLE BY RICK WOOD

CIA ROSE BOOK ONE

AFTER THE DEVIL HAS WON

RICK WOOD